TOM SWIFT AND HIS
ULTRASONIC CYCLOPLANE

THE NEW TOM SWIFT JR. ADVENTURES

BY VICTOR APPLETON II

A moment later the parachutist was safely inside the aeroplane

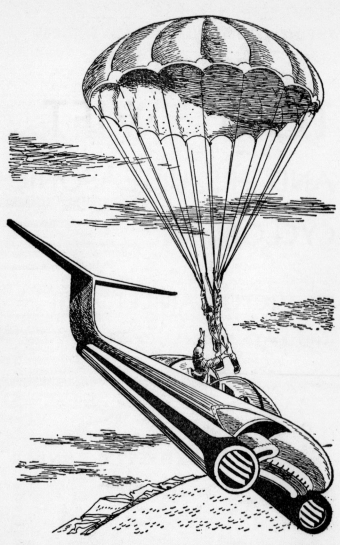

A moment later the parachutist was safely inside the cycloplane

THE NEW TOM SWIFT JR. ADVENTURES

TOM SWIFT

AND HIS ULTRASONIC CYCLOPLANE

BY VICTOR APPLETON II

ILLUSTRATED BY GRAHAM KAYE

NEW YORK

GROSSET & DUNLAP PUBLISHERS

PRINTED IN THE UNITED STATES OF AMERICA

CONTENTS

TOM SWIFT AND HIS
ULTRASONIC CYCLOPLANE

Tongues of fire darted up Tom's shop apron!

CHAPTER I

THE WEIRD FIGURE

"YOU mean this little gadget can rev up a big enough storm to fly your new cycloplane?"

Through the greenish quartz-glass window of his protective helmet, Bud Barclay stared in amazement at his pal, Tom Swift.

The young inventor chuckled. "An *ultrasonic* storm, Bud. You can't see it or hear it, but it packs a terrific wallop!"

The two eighteen-year-olds and Hank Sterling, the blond, rugged chief patternmaker of Swift Enterprises, were in Tom's private laboratory, testing a small ultrasonic generator which Tom had designed. All three wore special fiber-glass helmets and gauntlets to protect them from the dangerous but invisible pulsations of silent energy.

"As the electric current oscillates, this device beams out intensely powerful sound waves—far above the range of human hearing," Tom explained.

1

All eyes focused on the gleaming steel cylinder which housed the generator.

"Sure looks harmless enough," Bud remarked.

"Don't let its looks fool you, fly boy!" Tom retorted. "Those ceramic disks in there are vibrating over five million times a second. With waves of that frequency, you can—"

"*Tom! Look out!*"

The sudden yell of warning came from Hank Sterling on the other side of the workbench. As he spoke, he flicked off the master switch on the electrical control panel.

Glancing down, Tom saw a jagged tongue of fire dart up his shop apron. A second later the whole apron front burst into flames.

"Smokin' rockets!" gulped Bud.

Hank vaulted over the workbench to help Tom beat out the flames. But Bud acted even quicker.

Grabbing the laboratory fire extinguisher off the wall, he upended the tank and sprayed Tom with a lather of chemical foam which instantly doused the flames.

"Th-thanks, Bud—and you too, Hank!"

Shuddering with relief, the young scientist sank down on a laboratory stool and pulled off his helmet. Hank and Bud followed suit.

"Whew! A close call!" Tom muttered, managing a sickly grin. His face was pale and clammy with perspiration. Hank helped him remove the blackened remains of his shop apron.

"Sure you're all right, pal?" Bud demanded anxiously. Tom nodded and Bud chuckled. "I always knew your inventions were hot stuff, genius boy, but not *that* hot!"

The stocky, dark-haired youth heaved a sigh. "All kidding aside. What made your apron catch fire?" Bud asked in a puzzled voice.

"The ultrasonic waves," Tom replied ruefully. "All that concentrated energy heated the cotton fabric right up to the kindling point. I told you these high-frequency vibrations were dangerous!"

"Want to go on with the test, skipper?" asked Hank.

Tom shook his head. "Not now, Hank—I've had it for this morning. Before we do any more work on the ultrasonic generator, we'd better have some fireproof suits made of asbestalon."

"I'll take care of it pronto!" Hank promised.

The phone rang. Tom scooped up the receiver. "Tom Swift Jr. speaking."

"This is Dad, son," came a quiet voice over the line. "I've just had some interesting news. Can you come over to the office?"

"Sure thing, Dad—right away!"

After cleaning up a bit and changing his jersey, Tom hurried out of the laboratory and hopped into a jeep. Gunning the engine, he threw in the clutch and went roaring off across the grounds of Swift Enterprises.

This four-mile-square enclosure, crisscrossed with airstrips, was the experimental station where the famous father-and-son team of scientists developed their new inventions.

A few minutes later Tom strode into the big

modernistic office in the main building, which he shared with his father.

In addition to the huge desks, drawing board, and comfortable leather lounge chairs, the office contained models of many of the Swifts' greatest inventions. Among them were a silver, needle-nosed replica of Tom's *Star Spear,* the rocket ship in which he had pioneered a successful journey into outer space, and a blue plastic model of the jetmarine, a craft which he had used in hunting down a ring of undersea pirates.

"What's up, Dad?"

Tom Swift Sr. turned from his work with a smile. There was a close resemblance between father and son, especially noticeable in their deep-set blue eyes and clean-cut features, although Tom Jr. was the taller and rangier of the two.

"Sit down, son. You remember Cousin Ed Longstreet?"

"Sure do!" Tom grinned as he settled his lanky frame into a deep-cushioned green leather chair. "What far corner of the globe is he poking into these days?"

"I haven't kept up with his latest travels. But here—read this wire."

Tom took the telegram which his father handed him. Datelined Chicago that morning, it said:

> ARRIVING SHOPTON AIRPORT 2:30 P.M. TODAY. AM BRINGING SOMETHING UNU-SUAL WHICH I WOULD LIKE YOU BOTH TO EXAMINE.
>
> ED LONGSTREET

" 'Something unusual'?" Tom's forehead puckered into a frown. "What do you suppose it is, Dad?"

Mr. Swift shrugged and replied with a chuckle, "Haven't the faintest idea. But knowing Cousin Ed, it might be anything from a shrunken head to a new species of tropical butterfly!"

As Tom burst into laughter, the elder scientist added, "The point is, I'm taking off for The Citadel right after lunch. Could you meet him?"

"Sure—be glad to, Dad."

The Citadel was the Swifts' atomic energy plant in the Southwest. Research work for the government required frequent trips there from Shopton in the East, where Swift Enterprises was located.

Promptly at 2:27 that afternoon, Tom and Bud Barclay arrived at the Shopton airport. In order to carry an extra passenger, they had taken Bud's red convertible instead of Tom's two-seater sports car.

Moments later, a big silver air liner swooped in for a landing and discharged its passengers. Tom pointed to a slender, bareheaded figure coming down the ramp.

Ed Longstreet was a slightly built man, about twenty-five years old, with blond, thinning hair.

"Sorry Dad couldn't be here," Tom apologized, after introducing Bud and explaining Mr. Swift's absence. "But what's all this about a mysterious object you want us to examine?" he added with a twinkle.

"Right here in my brief case," Ed replied.

"You can examine it when we get to the plant."

On the way back to Swift Enterprises, Tom chatted with his cousin. From their conversation, Bud learned that Ed was a world traveler, a dabbler in various fields of science, and an expert linguist.

When they arrived at Tom's office, Ed Longstreet opened his brief case and took out a strange figurine. About twelve inches high, its shape was half human, half animal. The queer object shimmered with a beautiful yellow-orange iridescence.

"What is it?" asked Bud, staring in fascination.

"That's what I'm hoping Tom can tell me."

"Looks like some kind of primitive animal god," Tom remarked in a slow, puzzled voice. "Where'd you get it, Ed?"

"Picked it up in a San Francisco curio shop on my way back from South America," his cousin replied.

The young inventor pointed to the figure's kangaroolike stomach pouch. "Some kind of a marsupial, apparently. That may mean it came from the South Pacific area, somewhere around Australia."

"What's it made of?" Bud inquired.

Tom shook his head, pinching his lower lip thoughtfully. "That's what has me stumped. So far as I recall, I've never seen any substance quite like this. . . . Of course this yellow-orange color may indicate some kind of an oxide, due to weathering."

With his fingernail, Tom scratched the bottom

of the figure slightly, then hefted and tapped the object, noting its metallic ring.

"Wait a minute!" he exclaimed suddenly. "I may be wrong, but I've got a hunch about this. Let's hop over to my lab."

Using one of Enterprises' jeeps, they drove to Tom's all-glass private laboratory. Here the young inventor examined the statue quickly under a spectroscope. When he raised his head from the instrument, his blue eyes sparkled with excitement.

"Well, give out, genius boy!" urged Bud tensely. "What is it?"

"It's an ore of holmium—pure holmia—one of the rare earths!" Tom replied.

Bud's face remained blank. "Rare earths? What are they?"

"A group of very rare metals with tongue-twisting names like dysprosium, praseodymium, ytterbium—"

"Okay, okay, professor!" Bud put in hastily. "Just tell us what's so unusual about them."

"For one thing, they practically never occur in ore deposits all by themselves—at least not so far as modern science knows," Tom explained. "Ordinarily they have to be separated, in tiny quantities, from other substances like monazite sand, which is used in atomic energy production."

"Then where would the primitive people who made this statue get a whole hunk of this stuff?" Bud demanded.

"Good question. I wish I knew!"

"Does holmium have any value, aside from being so rare?" Ed Longstreet asked.

"Yes," Tom replied. "It can be used in making alloys, special glass and electronic parts, not to mention its various hush-hush applications. And scientists could probably find a lot more uses if there were a large enough supply."

"Hey!" Bud exclaimed, bouncing off his laboratory stool. "Then, if we could find out where this object came from, it might lead to a valuable uranium strike—I mean a rare earths strike!"

Tom nodded.

"Afraid I can't be of much help," said Ed. "I questioned the curio-shop owner, but the only thing he could tell me was that it arrived in a consignment of art objects he'd bought at auction."

Tom drummed his fingers thoughtfully on the workbench. "Maybe an art expert could help us."

Picking up the phone, he put through a long-distance call to Grandyke University. He spoke with Professor Feeney, a specialist in Oceanian art, who promised to come out and examine the strange figure. Tom then contacted Dr. Gorde, the curator of the Shopton Museum. The next day, both men arrived and studied the statue closely, but neither could offer any clue as to its exact origin. It might be Asiatic, Polynesian, or Melanesian.

"Most unusual example of primitive sculpture I've ever seen!" declared Dr. Gorde. "Would you permit the figure to be placed on display for a few days?"

Ed Longstreet, who was planning to fly on to New York, agreed willingly, so the statue was transported to the Shopton Museum. Radio and TV commentators mentioned the news item and the *Shopton Evening Bulletin* carried a front-page story about the queer pagan idol.

As a result, crowds stormed the museum the next day, eager to view the mysterious object. Armed guards were posted around the glass case in which the figure was displayed.

"It certainly caused a stir in town," Tom said to his blond, blue-eyed sister Sandra. He repeated this later to his slim, pretty mother when he kissed her good night.

Shortly after midnight, he was awakened by the shrill ringing of his bedside phone. Lifting the receiver sleepily, Tom asked who was calling.

"It's Dr. Gorde, Tom!" gasped a trembling voice. "The animal god has been stolen!"

CHAPTER II

JAKE THE CAT

THE NEWS shocked Tom wide awake. "Where are you calling from?" he asked quickly.

"Police Headquarters."

"Be right down!"

Tom dressed hurriedly and in a few minutes was backing his sports car out of the garage. A short time later he braked to a halt in front of Shopton Police Headquarters.

Shoving past reporters, he strode to the office of Police Chief Slater. Here he found Dr. Gorde and two night watchmen from the museum being questioned by detectives.

"Glad you're here, Tom," the chief greeted him. "Maybe you can give us some help on this."

"Exactly what happened?" Tom inquired.

A plain-clothes sergeant and the two night watchmen gave him a quick fill-in. The first hint of trouble had come with a sound of shattering glass in the east wing of the museum about 11:35 P.M. One of the watchmen had run to investigate, only to be knocked out by a blow on the head. A livid bruise still showed on his right temple.

The other watchman, arriving on the scene a minute or so later, had found the display case smashed and the mysterious figurine missing.

"What about the burglar alarm?" Tom asked.

"We checked that," the plain-clothes man reported. "Turned out someone had disconnected it from the inside—probably earlier in the evening, while the place was full of people. Then, after the museum was cleared and locked up for the night, he broke in through a high rear window."

"Any clues from the M.O.?" Tom asked.

"The M.O.?" put in Dr. Gorde, peering through his gold-rimmed pince-nez with a puzzled expression.

"The crook's *modus operandi,* or method of operation," the chief explained. "Yes, Tom, as a matter of fact, everything points to a well-known second-story man called Jake the Cat. Here—"

He leafed open a large rogues' gallery album on his desk, shoved it toward Tom, and pointed to two "mug shots"—front and side views—of a lean-faced, dark-haired man about thirty years old.

"That's the guy I'm talking about. He's been in and out of the penitentiary in half a dozen states for similar crimes. He specializes in thefts from public buildings and always kills the alarm first."

"But why on earth would a criminal of his type steal such an exquisite art object?" Dr. Gorde demanded.

"Art objects bring plenty of dough, don't they?" said Sergeant Camp, the plain-clothes man.

"Surely not in this case," the curator insisted. "Why, the statue must be known throughout the country by now, from all the news stories about it! Where could the thief dispose of it?"

"I agree with Dr. Gorde," Tom said. "No fence will handle stolen goods unless he can resell them at a profit. And I doubt if any private collector would dare to buy such an easily recognized item."

"*Hmmm.*" Chief Slater frowned and stroked his chin. "What's the angle then, Tom? Did Jake bungle this time?"

"Not necessarily. That statue is made of a very rare metal. If this Jake melted it down, it could never be recognized, but its industrial research value would still be worth thousands of dollars!"

"We'll contact the FBI and put out a dragnet for him," the chief promised.

The next morning Tom was hard at work on his cycloplane in one of the Enterprises hangars. Bud was with him.

"What's that box you're installing, skipper? Some kind of electronic gear?"

"It's a cybertron, Bud," the young inventor replied. "You've heard of cybernetics, the science of thinking machines? Well, this is a cyber*tron.*"

Bud looked baffled. "You mean that gadget does the thinking for the plane? Oh, I get it! Must be some kind of automatic pilot!"

"Right," said Tom. "A very advanced type of automatic pilot."

As Bud climbed up into the cockpit beside him, the young inventor explained how the cybertron, and gyrostabilizer, controlled by servo-mechanisms, would regulate the speed, course, and altitude of the cycloplane in flight. In addition, it would also beam out a radar-type signal to detect any obstacles in the plane's path.

"If an echo bounces back," Tom went on, "the cybertron automatically figures out what has to be done, and instantly alters the plane's course to avoid a crash."

"Wow! Wait'll the airlines get hold of that!"

"They'll have it soon, I hope," Tom replied with quiet pride. "That is, if it works out okay in my new cycloplane."

Bud's eyes roved over the nearly completed ship, noting its sleek yet fantastic design. "How's she coming, skipper?"

"Be ready for a flight test this afternoon. Want to sign on as copilot?"

"Do I!" Bud gave a joyful whoop. "Think I want to miss out on Professor Swift's latest and most revolutionary advance in the science of aviation? Only one thing I'm wondering," he added with a straight face. "Will it fly?"

Tom grinned. "We'll find out this afternoon."

On each side of the ship a shiny magnesium cylinder, wide as an oil drum, ran the full length of the fuselage. In flight, the twin cylinders would

spin at terrific speed, powered by Tom's ultrasonic generator which had now passed all tests
successfully.

"Do you really think those twin rollers will
provide enough lift for take-off and flight?" Bud
inquired doubtfully.

"They will if my answers to certain aerodynamic equations are correct. For example, when
you apply Bernoulli's equation—"

"Give it to me in kindergarten talk," Bud
pleaded. "Those ten-syllable words make my head
spin. And I'm not even air-borne yet!"

"Okay." Tom chuckled. "Know how a pitcher
throws a curve?"

"Sure—by making the ball spin."

"Right. And as the ball spins, it drags air
around it by surface friction. As a result, air piles
up on one side of the ball and thins out on the
other side."

Bud's face brightened as he suddenly caught
on. "Oh sure. That air build-up on one side
causes an increase in pressure, and that's what
forces the ball away from a straight-line path.
Only I still don't see what all that's got to do
with the twin cylinders on your cycloplane."

"Same principle. A stream of air from the
sonic turbine flows outward from the plane and
passes over the cylinder. As the cylinders spin
around, the air piles up on the lower surface.
So you get an increase in pressure there, just like
the pressure on the lower surface of a wing. And
that's what boosts us upstairs!"

"Guess it figures at that." Bud nodded slowly. "Will your cycloplane be able to do the same kind of flying as a helicopter—I mean, hovering and all?"

"Sure, but it'll also have many advantages over an ordinary helicopter," Tom pointed out. "For example, no overhead rotors to cope with, and no noise or vibration. With the ultrasonic generator powered by Swift solar-charged batteries, the plane will fly almost forever without new fuel. And with a jet engine added for forward flight, I'm hoping to break the sound barrier."

"Looks as if you'd picked the wrong name, skipper," Bud remarked. "Should be a *cyclocopter,* meaning a mixture of helicopter and cyclone!"

By this time, the mechanics had installed metal fairing at several points, thus smoothing the whole ship into sleek, unbroken lines from stem to stern.

Bud climbed down from the flight compartment and strolled around the ship, eying it from every angle.

"With the landing gear down, it looks like a racing land cruiser," he remarked.

"It *is* a land cruiser." Tom chuckled. "I forgot to tell you—this front landing wheel is for steering, of course, but the two rear wheels have a mechanical drive system. So, you see, the ship can be operated on land like a car!"

Bud whistled. "Man, oh man, if this baby could only cook, she'd have everything!"

Shortly after luncheon, the cycloplane was

wheeled out onto an airstrip. The two boys climbed aboard, wearing heavy flight gear in case of any emergencies during the test.

The roomy cabin contained both front and rear seats like an automobile. Tom and Bud took their places forward as pilot and copilot, then the canopy was closed and sealed.

This trial run was first in a series of five which proved satisfactory. During the next several days a few kinks were ironed out. At last the boys were ready to give the craft its major test—trying to break the sound barrier.

"Going to use the jet on take-off?" Bud inquired.

Tom shook his head. "No. We'll take the express elevator straight upward. Hang onto your hat, pal. Here goes!"

Switching on the ultrasonic generator, Tom cut in the rotor drums. With a smooth purr, the twin cylinders spun into action. Slowly at first, then with dizzying speed, the cycloplane rose into the blue.

"Wow, what a climb!" Bud gasped, shooting a glance at the indicator. "Eight thousand feet a minute!"

Below them, Swift Enterprises with its sprawling buildings had dwindled away to toy size. The whole of Shopton and the blue expanse of Lake Carlopa were partly hidden by cloud banks and floating haze.

"Now let's give 'er the gun!" Tom chuckled, well-pleased by the ship's performance so far.

He opened the jet to full power. As the craft shot forward, he kicked in the afterburner. Like a rocket, the ship speared through the blue!

"We'll climb a bit higher, then dive through the sound barrier," Tom announced. "Probably wouldn't hurt to pick up a bit more altitude before we—"

His words were cut short as the plane bucked suddenly in a violent shudder. The next instant, both boys were shaken by wave after wave of crazy vibrations that raced through the fuselage as the ship careened wildly out of control!

"G-good night! D-do something, s-s-skipper!" Bud pleaded.

With a desperate effort, Tom slammed shut the jet throttle. Instantly the air-speed indicator flickered downward.

The vibrations slowly died away and the ship steadied on course. Tom brought her around in a gentle turn and began a long glide back to Shopton.

"Good night! What happened?" Bud asked.

"Not sure." The young inventor frowned. "But I have a pretty good idea."

"Name it."

"The ultrasonic waves from the generator interfere with the normal air flow. At low speeds it's not noticeable, but somewhere around 450 knots, it sets up a violent disturbance."

Picking out the closest landing spot, Tom reported his predicament to the control tower and came down on the commercial airfield at the

Swift Construction Company. This company, managed by Mr. Swift's boyhood chum and business associate, Ned Newton, manufactured the various inventions which Tom and his father developed at Swift Enterprises.

"Whew!" Bud heaved a deep sigh of relief as the ship rolled to a halt on the concrete. "For a while there, I thought we were goners for sure!"

Tom looked grim but said nothing as he climbed out of the cabin. Doffing his flight gear, he made a careful check of the whole cycloplane. As he had feared, structural failures had occurred at several points.

Bud studied his pal's face, tight-lipped with disappointment. "What's the answer, chum?"

Tom shrugged. "I'll have to find some way to keep those ultrasonic waves from being transmitted through the whole air frame. Maybe I can do this by installing a different kind of mount for the power unit. I'll start working on one."

"Hey, there's Sandy!" Bud exclaimed. He pointed to a girl and a man emerging from a small, sleek private plane which had just landed. "Guess she's been demonstrating one of your Pigeon Specials."

Tom's sister Sandy, a year younger than her brother, was a skillful pilot. Both Tom and Mr. Swift had given her many hours of expert flying instruction.

Seeing the two boys, Sandy walked over and introduced her customer to them. "This is

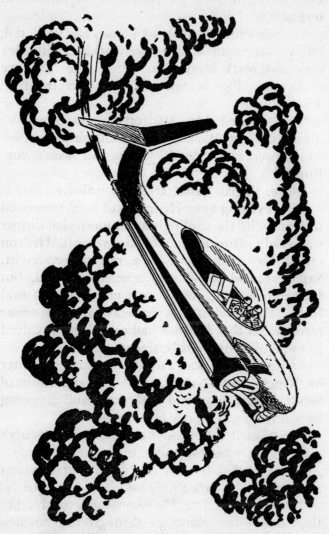

The ship, out of control, careened wildly

George Hedron—he's thinking of buying one of our new models."

Hedron smiled and shook hands. He was a tall, lanky young man of about twenty-three, with dark eyes and black wavy hair. "Fine little pleasure craft, that Pigeon Special," he complimented Tom.

"I've invited Mr. Hedron to our house to dinner tonight. We can talk about the purchase," Sandy went on. "You'll come too, won't you, Bud?"

"Sure, thanks," Bud accepted quickly.

That evening after Hedron had been presented to Mrs. Swift, she smilingly announced that dinner was ready. During the delicious meal, Hedron talked about his work as a research zoologist. Sandy seemed to be very much impressed, but Bud watched the young man narrowly and said little. The copilot was harassed by the vague recollection that Hedron had once been involved in some unscrupulous business transaction.

Another guest was Phyllis Newton, daughter of "Uncle Ned" Newton, and a school chum of Sandy's. Phyl, who had dark curls and laughing brown eyes, was Tom's favorite date.

"Looks as if Bud doesn't think much of Sandy's guest," she whispered to Tom after dinner.

The zoologist left the party first. As Bud was about to go, he took Sandy aside and said quietly:

"Please don't date Hedron again, Sandy. Let the sale of the plane go through the business office. He's not for you!"

CHAPTER III

DISTRESS SIGNAL

AS BUD hurried off, Sandy stared in surprise. What was wrong with George Hedron? Returning to Phyl, she told her of Bud's parting remarks.

"I wouldn't worry about it," said Phyl. With a giggle she added, "I do believe Bud's jealous, Sandy!"

Next morning, Bud was still scowling when he strode into Tom's private laboratory. "Skipper," he began, "I think we should check up on that guy Hedron—"

"Hold it, fly boy!" Tom interrupted with a smile. "Before you go any farther, how'd you like to fly to New Guinea?"

"New Guinea!" Bud's mouth dropped open in sheer amazement. "That's way down in the South Pacific near Australia!"

"I know. We just got an urgent order from a gold mine down there—in Dutch New Guinea, to be exact." Tom waved a radiogram he had been reading.

21

"An order for what?"

"Half a dozen Swift solar batteries. The mine's generators keep breaking down, due to the tropical climate. So now they've decided to use solar batteries to power all their mining equipment."

Tom's solar batteries, one of his most successful operations, stored up intense energy from the sun's rays in a small compact unit. The batteries were manufactured on a production line in Tom's sky-wheel man-made satellite, known as his Outpost in Space.

"The mine needs the batteries pronto and they're willing to pay for fast delivery," Tom added.

Bud scanned the radiogram quickly. "Wow, what an assignment! How soon do we take off?"

"Not we—I'll have to stay here and design those new engine mounts for the cycloplane," Tom explained, grinning at his pal's eagerness. "But Hank Sterling will go along to install the batteries and trouble-shoot the setup."

"It's a deal!"

Within two hours a cargo jet had been checked and fueled for the long overseas flight. Waving good-by to Tom and the ground crew, Bud and Hank climbed aboard.

"Have a good trip, fellows!" Tom shouted.

"Thanks! Cheerio!"

"And watch out for those head-hunters!" joked a mechanic.

A short time later came the signal for take-off.

With Bud at the controls, the big jet roared down the runway and climbed steeply into the blue. As the plane dwindled to a speck in the south-western sky, a voice boomed over the loud-speaker mounted above the communications building:

"Tom Swift, please contact your secretary at once!" Tom hurried to the main building of Swift Enterprises. Miss Trent, cool and efficient, greeted him at her desk outside the big double office.

"A call from Police Headquarters."

Tom rushed into his office and grabbed up the phone. "Tom Swift Jr. speaking."

"This is Chief Slater, Tom. We've picked up Jake the Cat. Want to help us question him?"

"I sure do! Give me fifteen minutes to get there!"

In his low-slung silver sports car, Tom made good time to Police Headquarters. In the chief's office, Jake the Cat sat handcuffed on a hard, straight-backed chair under a bright light. The swarthy burglar, wearing a high-necked jersey, looked as lean and agile as a trapeze stunt man.

"Has he confessed?" Tom asked, after the chief had introduced him to the detectives who had captured the prisoner.

"Sure—I'll spill the whole story!" Jake whined. "Just gimme a break at the trial, that's all I ask!"

"We're not making any promises," snapped Chief Slater. "Those fingerprints you forgot to wipe off the burglar alarm give us a clear-cut case. But go ahead and talk, and we'll tell the judge you co-operated."

"Okay, okay. Whaddaya want to know?"

"Where's that statue you stole?"

"I ain't got it. I turned it over to the guy who hired me to pull the job."

"The guy who hired you!" Chief Slater glowered in surprise. "What do you mean?"

"Just what I'm tellin' ya," Jake insisted. "This guy calls me on the phone the other night, and offers me a nice little bundle of cash to snatch the statue from the museum."

"Who was he?" Tom asked.

"Search me. I never even seen his face."

"Don't give us that!" growled Chief Slater. "You must have seen him when you turned over the statue."

"Sure, but he was wearin' a mask. On top of that, he made me meet him down by the docks where it was pitch black. I'm tellin' ya, this guy was plenty cagey!"

The chief shot a puzzled glance at Tom. There was a brief silence.

"Do you think he's telling the truth?" the young inventor asked.

One of the detectives shrugged. "Could be. We searched his rooms with a fine-tooth comb and couldn't find any trace of the stolen statue. But Jake was sporting a big bank roll."

Tom turned back to the prisoner. "Tell us anything you noticed about this man who hired you."

Jake knit his brows thoughtfully. "Well, he was about medium size. And I figgered he might be some kind of foreigner."

"Why?"

"He pronounced his J's funny. Like for instance, he called me 'Zhake' instead of Jake."

"*Hmm.* Not much of a clue," Tom commented, "but at least it's something to go on."

"We'll follow it up," Chief Slater promised. After hammering a few more questions at the prisoner, he nodded to the detectives. "Okay, take him away!"

Two days later, while Tom was busy in his private laboratory, perfecting the new engine mounts, the phone rang. Answering it, he heard the urgent voice of Swift Enterprises' electronics chief.

"This is George Dilling, Tom. I'm in the radio room. Bud and Hank are in trouble! They took off an hour ago for the return trip and ran into a terrific local storm over the jungle."

A surge of fear swept over Tom. "Are you getting their signal?"

"Yes. They're on the air right now."

"Okay. I'm on my way!"

Slamming down the phone, Tom dashed outside to his jeep, sped to the communications building, and raced upstairs to the radio room.

"The message is actually coming from the West Coast," Dilling explained as he handed Tom a set of earphones. "Ted Elheimer's picking it up out there and relaying it back to Shopton."

Elheimer was the California telecaster in the Swifts' private communications network.

As Tom adjusted the earphones, he heard Bud's voice saying, "Repeat position: latitude three degrees, fifty-eight minutes south, longitude one-thirty-six—"

Suddenly the young flier's voice broke off with a gasp. Then again it came crackling over the earphones:

"Something's wrong! The instruments have gone haywire! *We're going to crash!*"

With a loud crackle of static, the broadcast cut out completely!

CHAPTER IV

RESCUE FLIGHT

"BUD!" Tom shouted frantically. "Bud, can you read me? . . . Shopton calling Swift Jet Four!" There was no reply except the sputter of static.

Ripping off his earphones, Tom darted to the videophone and flipped on the switch. As the screen lighted up, Ted Elheimer's face came into view.

"What happened to the signal, Ted?" the young inventor cried out. "Any trouble in the relay hookup?"

Elheimer shook his head gloomily. "No, Tom. The transmission just stopped, that's all. I'm afraid they must have crashed."

"Crashed?" Dilling echoed the word in dismay. "Good night, in country like that, they won't stand a chance! Mountains and jungles are bad enough, but those natives are head-hunters, aren't they?"

"Some of them are." Tom clenched his jaw grimly. "The important thing is, Bud and Hank may have parachuted to safety. They'll be depending on us!"

Tom hurried back to his office and immediately began organizing a rescue expedition. Issuing orders at high speed, he dictated a number of memos to Miss Trent, then phoned the news to his mother.

Mrs. Swift was extremely proud of her husband and son. She found it difficult, however, not to be fearful of the dangers they often encountered while pursuing their scientific work.

"Oh dear," she murmured. "Please be careful, son. A rescue flight to uncharted jungle country is dreadfully risky!"

"Don't worry, Mother," Tom soothed her. "I won't take any unnecessary chances, but I certainly can't leave Bud and Hank in the lurch."

"Of course you can't, my dear, and I'm very glad you feel that way. I'll be praying for a safe return for all of you!"

To transport the rescue expedition, Tom had chosen his huge atomic-powered aircraft, the *Sky Queen*. This mammoth ship, nicknamed the Flying Lab, had been designed by the young inventor to help him carry out scientific research work in any part of the globe.

At the underground hangar where the *Queen* was berthed, Tom beamed an electronic key to open the door and descended a wide staircase of burnished steel. On the floor below, there was a bustle of activity. Mechanics swarmed over the mighty three-decker craft, which filled the entire underground hangar space with its swept-back silver wings.

"Engines all check?" Tom asked the crew chief.

"Not yet, skipper. Couple of burned out units. We should have her all loaded and ready for take-off by five o'clock."

"Good work. Buzz me as soon as you're ready, Slim." Tom turned to go when a loud, gravelly voice came booming down the stairs:

"Gangway, you cowpokes an' buckaroos! Gimme lots o' room now! Here comes the grub!"

For a moment it looked as though a whole supermarket had grown a pair of bowlegs and was clumping downstairs under its own power. The legs were clad in blue denims, stuffed into high-heeled cowboy boots. Above, the rest of the figure was blocked from view by an enormous carton, loaded high with groceries and canned foods.

"Gangway, all you waddies! Chuck wagon's comin' down, so—"

"*Chow!*" Tom let out a yell as he saw one of the man's boots miss a step.

The next instant, cans, bottles, blue denims, boots and all came tumbling and clattering head-long down the steel stairs!

There was a moment of stunned silence as the echoes died away and the cans and assorted objects stopped rolling and came to rest. Then a stout, weather-beaten figure emitted a faint groan and raised itself painfully from the debris.

"Chow, are you all right?" Tom gasped as he hurried to assist the middle-aged Westerner.

"Don't reckon I'll know till I try standin' up. Here, gimme a hand, son."

Tom slipped a shoulder under one arm while Slim Davis, the crew chief, supported Chow on

The next instant, Chow and the groceries

the other side. Together, they managed to hoist the bald-headed, roly-poly man to his feet.

Gingerly Chow Winkler tested his limbs. A former chuck-wagon cook, he had met the Swifts on one of their trips to the Southwest, and had become so attached to Tom that he had come East to Shopton. Now private chef for the Swifts at Enterprises, he accompanied the young inventor on most of his expeditions.

The Texan grinned wanly. "Left eye feels like I might wind up with a shiner. Mebbe I better slap on a hunk o' beefsteak jest in case."

"Don't bother, Chow," a mechanic guffawed. "With that shirt you're wearing, who'll notice your eyes?"

came tumbling down the steel stairs

Forgetting all about his bruises, Chow turned from side to side to display his purple and flame-orange cowboy shirt.

"Ain't it a jim-dandy?" he beamed. "I picked up this here lil ole number in San Antone on my—"

A phone rang shrilly at the rear of the hangar. "It's for you, skipper!" a mechanic sang out.

Tom hurried back to take the call.

"This is George Hedron," said the voice at the other end of the line. "I just heard the news from Sandy about your rescue expedition, so I decided to call up and volunteer."

"Volunteer?" Tom was puzzled for a moment.

"To go with you. You see, I've been down in the New Guinea jungles before, collecting specimens. I might be able to help you a good bit."

"Oh, I see." Remembering Bud's warning about Hedron, Tom stalled. "It's kind of you to offer, but I'm not sure that we'll be able to take another person. May I call you back?"

"Sure, you can reach me here all afternoon," Hedron replied, and gave Tom his phone number.

After hanging up, Tom frowned for a moment, then dialed Harlan Ames, the plant security chief at Swift Enterprises. Quickly he told what he knew of Hedron's background and Bud's uneasiness about him.

"Check up on Hedron, will you, Harlan? Find out if he's on the up-and-up, and call me back as soon as possible."

"Will do, Tom!"

In less than an hour Ames reported back. "Everything looks all right, Tom. I checked Hedron's university record and he holds a master's degree in zoology. The medical lab where he's employed claims he's a first-rate scientist, and has been in Dutch New Guinea. So far as I can find out on short notice, he has no criminal record."

"Good enough, Harlan. Thanks!"

Tom felt that there was now no reason to turn down Hedron's offer of assistance, especially in such a life-and-death emergency. So he phoned the zoologist and told him to prepare for immediate departure.

Soon after five o'clock, the roof of the underground hangar swung open in two halves, rotated by smooth-working gears. The hangar floor was then raised to ground level by hydraulic lifts, and a rubber-tired tractor pulled the *Sky Queen* out onto the special runway for take-off.

Sandy and Phyl Newton had driven out to the plant to wish Tom a last-minute farewell. "I'll be worried every minute you're gone," Phyl confessed shyly, "so do be careful!"

"I promise." Tom smiled, then blushed as Phyl raised herself on tiptoe and gave him a quick kiss.

Sandy was tearful. "Tom, watch out. And you *must* find Bud—and Hank, too!"

Tom gave his sister a gentle squeeze. "Don't worry, Sis. We'll bring 'em both back safely."

One by one, the members of the rescue party climbed aboard the giant plane. Besides Chow, Hedron, and Slim Davis, there was Arvid Hanson, the expert modelmaker of Swift Enterprises who was also a crack pilot, and Doc Simpson, the young plant physician. Four flight crewmen made up the rest of the expedition.

In the flight compartment, Tom settled himself in the pilot's seat and ran through a quick instrument checkoff. Then, after clearing with the control tower and waving to the two girls, he gunned the nuclear engines. With a mighty roar the *Sky Queen* shot straight up, then soared ahead.

Streaking across the continent at over twelve hundred miles an hour, Tom and his companions saw a tapestry of farm land, cities, plains, and mountains unroll beneath them. Then came the long flight across the billowing blue-green waters of the Pacific.

Occasionally they passed over tiny ships trailing long wisps of smoke, or tropic atolls ringed by coral reefs and breakers of foam. Almost ten hours after leaving Shopton, the rescue party sighted New Guinea.

"We've outrun the sun," Arv Hanson commented.

Tom nodded, glancing at his watch. In the local time zone, it was only a few minutes before three o'clock in the afternoon!

Flying inland over the enormous island, they sighted dismal swamps, dense tropical rain forests, and towering mountain ranges. At some points, the ground was cleared in cultivated patches where the natives raised taro, yams, and vegetables. But most of the terrain appeared wild and forbidding.

"Have you pin-pointed the spot where the crash occurred?" a voice behind Tom asked.

Looking up from his map, he saw George Hedron entering the flight compartment.

"Should be right about here, according to the position Bud gave." Tom pointed toward the ground.

Hedron frowned doubtfully. "If Bud's instruments were going haywire, the position he gave was probably way off."

Pointing just ahead, he called Tom's attention to the fact that the area was blanketed by clouds. Hedron explained that fearful storms raged over this spot all the time.

"I think a few miles beyond would be a better place to land. The clear valley there will give us a chance to search in all directions. Besides," added the zoologist, "it's directly in Bud and Hank's line of flight on their way back from the gold fields."

"Okay, we'll try there first," Tom agreed.

Ten minutes later he swooped downward toward a rough clearing. Tom switched on the jet lifters and allowed the *Sky Queen* to settle gently onto the floor of the valley. There was no sign of habitation, but the land had definitely been cleared by human hands.

The big ship had hardly touched ground when the hatch opened and the men piled out. All were eager to explore the lush green surroundings.

"Sure didn't see no sign of any plane wreckage when we was comin' down," Chow reported gloomily.

"It might not be visible among the trees," Tom pointed out. "We'll split up into twos and scout around."

Tom drew Slim Davis as a companion. Together, they struck eastward through the forest. The air was spicy with the scent of tropical flowers, but insects were a constant nuisance. Overhead, the cries of strange birds broke the quiet of the jungle.

"Sure hope we don't meet up with any cannibals," Slim remarked jokingly. "Hey, what's—!"

He broke off with a gasp as he stumbled over a grassy hummock—a hummock which came to life! Rearing up on long, ostrichlike legs, it turned into a bird about five feet tall.

"Good night! What is it?" Slim goggled.

"Cassowary, I think." Tom chuckled, adding, "Look out! They're dangerous if they've been wounded!"

Evidently Slim had injured the cassowary. Shaking its wattles like an angry turkey cock, the big bird glared at the man. The creature's head was crested with a large, black horny helmet, and its unfeathered face and wrinkled neck were of scarlet, yellow, and purplish blue.

Suddenly the cassowary hurled itself at Slim!

With a yelp, he shinned up the nearest tree, while Tom, to be on the safe side, climbed another. Below the treed pair, the bird, beside itself with rage, stalked rapidly back and forth.

"Guess we'd better sit this one out," Tom called to Slim.

"You bet. Lucky thing that species sticks to the ground!"

Finally, with another vigorous shake of its wattles, the cassowary disappeared into the jungle. Tom and Slim sighed in relief and slid down from their perches. They continued the search, and when they reached higher ground, looked around hopefully. Still they detected no trace of the missing fliers.

"If Bud and Hank *were* nearby," said Tom, "we'd have spotted some sign of them from this point. Guess we'd better head back," he added, discouraged.

When they reached the ship, Tom and Slim found that the other searching teams had returned, with no better luck to report.

"Come on. Let's take off!" the young inventor decided. "We'll fly to the position Bud gave just before the crash."

With all hands aboard, Tom seated himself at the controls. He switched on the atomic engine and fed power to the jet lifters.

But the huge ship refused to rise off the ground!

CHAPTER V

JUNGLE ESCAPE

AS TOM pumped the throttle and checked all the instruments, Chow Winkler popped his bald head into the flight cabin.

"What's wrong?" the Texan queried. "Ain't we goin' to take off like you said, Tom?"

"We can't. For some reason the jet lifters aren't getting any power." Unhooking his seat belt, Tom added, "I'll go below and check."

Accompanied by Slim Davis and armed with a kit of tools, he hurried down a winding steel ladder to the first deck. Here the two trouble-shooters opened an inspection port and squeezed into the engine compartment.

"That Tomasite plastic your dad invented is sure a big help in this close-quarter work," Slim remarked, applying a wrench to a regulator nut.

Tom nodded. "It shields the reactor without wasting an inch of space."

This amazing plastic, besides being a good radiation shield, also had certain electromagnetic properties which prevented any homing shells or missiles from detonating.

An hour's check failed to disclose the cause of the trouble. Next, Tom inspected the jet lifters in the ship's underbelly. Slim joined him a few minutes later.

"Any luck?" Doc Simpson inquired, as they paused to wipe the dripping sweat off their brows.

Tom shook his head. "The tubes are clear. Must be something we missed in the engine compartment."

By this time, a purple dusk had descended over the trees. Night was coming on fast, and the screams and twitterings of the jungle birds died away to a faint murmur.

Grimly Tom surveyed the prospects ahead. What if the whole rescue expedition should find itself marooned in the wilderness? But he shook off the gloomy thought.

"Come an' get it, buckaroos!" Chow appeared in the doorway, banging a metal triangle. "How 'bout you an' Slim knockin' off fer now, Tom? Soup's on!"

Dinner proved a dismal meal, in spite of Chow's tasty cooking. As soon as Tom finished eating, he hurried up to the radio compartment and called Shopton. To his delight, his father's voice responded to the code signal.

"Just got back this evening and heard the news, son. Have you found any trace of Hank and Bud?"

"Not yet, Dad. I was hoping that they might have got a message through to Shopton."

"No. Dilling tells me he's had no further word since the crash. But here's a slight piece of good news, Tom. The police just called to report that they now have a lead on that masked stranger— the one who hired Jake the Cat to steal the statue."

"That's great, Dad. Glad to hear it."

In order not to worry his family or the relatives of his men, Tom decided to avoid any mention of engine trouble. After sending his love to his mother, Phyl, and Sandy, the young inventor said good-by.

Just as he switched off the transmitter, Chow came into the radio room on tiptoe. From the furtive way he peered into the passageway, it was obvious that he was bringing secret news.

"What's up, Chow?" Tom asked.

"Tom, do you reckon someone could have messed up this here airplane so it can't fly no more?"

"*Sabotage?* No, I never even considered that, Chow! Why?"

" 'Cause when I was hikin' back from the woods this afternoon, I heard some kind o' hammerin' noises. Sounded to me like they might have come from the *Sky Queen*."

Tom's pulse quickened with interest. "Did you see anyone near the plane?"

Chow shook his head. "Nope. When I got back, there warn't no one around, so I figgered I must have been mistook. But now I'm not so sure!"

Tom gave the roly-poly Texan's shoulder a pat of approval. "Thanks for telling me, Chow. I'll check right away!"

Calling the men together, the young inventor questioned each one carefully. But apparently no one had been out of sight of his fellow searcher long enough to do any mischief to the plane.

Tom was baffled. If none of his men was the saboteur, then who had been doing the hammering? Unfriendly natives, perhaps? Natives who had already captured Bud and Hank, and were even now keeping watch on the rescue party?

But wild tribesmen would have damaged the Flying Lab in some cruder fashion, Tom reflected. It was a mystifying problem.

"Just to be on the safe side, we'd better search the plane for stowaways," he announced. "Arv, you take charge, will you? Slim and I will go back to work on the engine."

Hanson responded with a quick salute, "Righto, skipper!"

Twenty minutes later he reported, "Tom, we've been over every inch of the ship. No one's hiding on board."

"Okay, Arv. Thanks." Tom laid down a beryllium wrench and wiped a smear of grease off his face with his sleeve. "By the way, we've spotted the trouble." He held up a length of copper tubing. It was part of the servo-control hookup to the jet-lifter throttle. "Someone crimped the line with a pair of pliers," he explained tersely.

Hanson's eyes widened in dismay. "Then it *was* sabotage!"

"No doubt about it. Whoever did this planned the whole thing ahead of time and installed a dummy fitting to hide the damage." Tom said no more, though he was greatly worried. A highly skilled technician, possibly a white man, was back of the sabotage.

After replacing the length of tubing, he took the *Sky Queen* up for a brief test flight. This time, the mammoth ship checked out perfectly. Since the jungle was now shrouded in darkness, Tom felt that further searching that day would be fruitless. They would continue in the morning. He brought the ship down and arranged for guards during the night. There were no visitors, however.

Mist still drifted among the trees when the *Sky Queen* soared aloft at dawn. With Slim as copilot, Tom headed eastward to the spot that Bud had indicated in his frantic radio call. For half an hour they cruised back and forth over the area without spotting the wreckage.

Finally Tom said, "I think our best bet is a storm area." Suddenly he pointed off to starboard, where a mass of dark clouds blotted out the landscape. "That may be it, Slim!"

Banking sharply, Tom steered straight for the area of heavy weather. As they plowed through the overcast, two towering volcanic peaks loomed up ahead!

Chow, who had come forward to the flight

compartment with Hedron and two other members of the rescue party, gulped nervously. "Brand my ripcord, I sure hope you know where you're goin', Tom!"

"Bud and Hank may have crashed between those peaks or just beyond," Tom replied coolly. "I want a closer look."

As they entered the turbulent storm area, the giant ship began to buck and shudder violently. Tom seemed to lose control of the *Sky Queen*.

Chow yelled in panic, "We're goin' to crash!"

CHAPTER VI

BETWEEN VOLCANOES

THE FACES of Tom's crewmen blanched with alarm. But the young inventor managed to quiet their fears momentarily with his reply:

"Relax, Chow! If any ship can get through, the Flying Lab can."

"That's j-just what's worryin' me," the cook quavered. "Don't hardly look like anything bigger'n a hoot owl could fly betwixt those peaks!"

The plane was now at the very heart of the storm. Rain lashed the cabin windows, and the extinct volcanoes stood out in the leaden darkness like sentinels of doom. Tom was forced to jockey the craft like a balky horse to keep it aloft.

Cutting the forward jets, he braked the *Sky Queen* sharply. Then, as the plane lost momentum against the buffeting winds, Tom eased off on the jet lifter throttle. Slowly he began the dangerous descent into the gorge between the peaks.

"Everyone keep a lookout for signs of wreckage!" he instructed his companions.

His own eyes darted from side to side—conning the instrument dials, gauging the distance between the jagged and threatening mountain walls to port and starboard. So tightly was the mammoth plane boxed in by the peaks that again and again it seemed as if the buffeting winds would cause a disaster!

Beads of sweat glistened on Slim Davis's forehead as he watched Tom's icy-nerved maneuvers. "Only that boy could do it," he thought tensely.

Suddenly there was a screech of tortured metal and the whole ship rocked and vibrated under the impact.

"The left wing tip is scraping!" yelled Slim.

Instantly Tom yanked the throttle and poured power to the jet lifters. Like a rocket, the plane shot up from between the volcanoes, with a blast of smoke and flame.

Chow had collapsed into the nearest seat, his rotund bulk quivering with nervous shock. "Brand my sagebrush salad," he moaned, mopping his bald head with a red bandanna, "why don't we try somethin' safe fer a change?" He grimaced. "Like hirin' some head-hunters to give us all a good short haircut?"

"Sorry, Chow"—Tom repressed a worried grin—"but I'm afraid this jungle rescue business is going to be no picnic any way we tackle it!" Turning serious, he added, "Did any of you spot traces of Bud and Hank's plane?"

The others responded with a gloomy negative.

"Pretty tough to see much, though, with all

this overcast," commented Sam Barker, one of the flight crew. "We could have missed them easily."

Above the storm area now, Tom stared at the dark cloud masses billowing around the peaks.

"Guess we muffed our chance that time," he brooded. "With Dad's giant searchlight, we could have picked out ground details clearly."

This famous invention of Mr. Swift's was capable of illuminating large areas with the brilliance of strong sunshine.

"Jumpin' horned toads!" gulped Chow, turning pale beneath his desert tan. "You don't mean you're aimin' to try that loco stunt *again?*"

Tom shook his head. "No. We don't have a searchlight on board. Anyhow, it's no use trying to fly any lower in the *Sky Queen*—our wing span's too great."

"Are you giving up?" George Hedron inquired.

"Not by a long shot!" vowed the young inventor. "Slim, you make a landing somewhere and I'll try to get through in the *Kangaroo Kub*."

The *Kub*, a midget jet plane, was one of two pint-sized aircraft carried in the vast cargo hold of the Flying Lab. The other was a tiny helicopter called the *Skeeter*.

The jungle terrain below offered few open spaces large enough for landing the *Sky Queen*. The nearest spot was a valley, about fifteen miles from the slopes of the volcanoes. When they reached it, Tom said:

"That'll do. Take over, Slim."

Leaving his copilot at the controls, Tom

scrambled below to the ship's hangar space. A flick of a wall button opened the sliding aluminum doors of the rear cargo port.

Slipping into the cockpit of the *Kangaroo Kub,* Tom locked the canopy and hastily warmed up the engine.

"All set, Slim," he signaled into his mike.

With a *swoosh* the Flying Lab nosed upward in a steep climb. Tom fired a cartridge to release the chocks, and the tiny jet shot from the hangar.

Once air-borne, the *Kub* was steered back toward the pass. But almost as soon as Tom penetrated the storm area, he realized that the odds were hopeless.

Seized by the violent crosscurrents, the small craft was tossed and buffeted like a feather in a windstorm. Tom felt a wave of panic as the stubby jet failed to respond to its controls.

"I'd better cut back on the throttle!" Tom said to himself.

As the jet thrust slackened, the plane teetered perilously on the brink of a stall. Tom waited for the split-second bite as its controls took hold, then hauled up its nose and "poured on the coal." The *Kub* zoomed upward like a comet!

"Whew!" Tom felt his heart pounding with relief. "Well, there goes *that* idea!"

Disappointed but far from defeated, the young inventor streaked toward the jungle clearing where the *Sky Queen* had already landed. Slim and his flight crew had hastily rigged a special arresting gear, so Tom was able to set down the midget jet without trouble and let it roll into the hangar.

"Any luck?" Doc Simpson voiced the question of the whole group as Tom climbed out of the cockpit.

Tom shook his head glumly. "Not yet. The *Kub* wouldn't handle in the storm. But that doesn't mean we're licked. I'll try again—next time in the copter."

Whirling aloft in the *Skeeter* a few moments later, Tom headed back to the extinct volcanoes. This craft responded well on the fringes of the storm, but as Tom neared the center of turbulence between the peaks, the helicopter began to shudder violently. Tom's muscles ached from the strain of fighting the controls.

Built for short hops and delicate maneuvering, the *Skeeter* began to groan and screech under the battering punishment of the storm winds.

"A couple more minutes of this could tear the *Skeeter* apart!" Tom realized grimly.

Discouraged, he gave up and flew back to the landing spot. As the whirlybird settled to earth, Tom saw Arv Hanson clamber excitedly from the *Sky Queen's* hatch and come on a run to greet him.

"What's up?" Tom shouted, bursting out of the helicopter's cabin.

"Bud and Hank are alive—at least, one of them is!" Arv reported breathlessly as the other men clustered around. "I just picked up a faint broadcast on the ship's radio!"

CHAPTER VII

A DANGEROUS SEARCH

"YOU'RE SURE it was Bud or Hank?" Tom grabbed Hanson by the shoulders.

"Positive! The signal was pretty feeble, and there was too much static to recognize the voice. But it was one of our boys, all right! He must have used the transmitter in his parachute gear!"

"What did he say?"

Arv's face clouded. "I couldn't make out too well, but it sounded something like: *'Rare . . . like what you . . .'* That's all I could understand. Then the signal faded out completely."

"Did you try to call them back?" Tom asked eagerly.

"Sure. I've been trying ever since, but no response."

"Well, *keep* trying!"

As Hanson headed back to the *Sky Queen,* the other members of the rescue expedition pelted Tom with questions about the results of his flight in the *Skeeter.*

"I doubt if any type of aircraft could make a landing in that storm area," Tom told them. "Unless possibly," he added, with a thoughtful gleam in his eyes, "my new cycloplane could do it."

"But that's in Shopton," Slim pointed out. "And it's not even ready yet."

"I know." The young inventor brooded silently for a moment.

Red Jones, flight crewman, spoke up. "If an air rescue of Bud and Hank is out, what're we going to do?"

"Try reaching them overland," Tom decided. "Looks as if it's our only hope."

Unfortunately, the expedition's gear on board the *Sky Queen* included no complete outfits for a long jungle hike. But Tom refused to be intimidated by this obstacle.

"We'll get through, somehow," he told himself.

After consulting Hedron about possible hazards, he issued a number of orders. Then the young inventor hurried aboard the Flying Lab and interrupted Arv Hanson long enough to put through a radio call to Shopton.

"Any news, son?" Mr. Swift's voice came through the unscrambling device.

"Yes, and good news at that, Dad!" Tom quickly told his father about the signal which Hanson had picked up. "But there's some bad news, too," he went on. "We've spotted the place where Bud and Hank crashed, but there's no chance of landing—or even trying an air pickup. That means we'll have to reach them the hard way."

"Through the jungle?" The elder scientist's voice was tinged with worry.

"Right, Dad. We'll start out this afternoon."

"But, Tom, you're not equipped for a land search of that kind."

"I believe we can make out," Tom reassured him. "Anyhow, it's worth a try on foot first. If we can't get through, I may have to use the cycloplane. In my opinion, that aerodynamic principle offers our only chance of stable flight in such a turbulent sky as this one."

"*Hmm,* you may be right, son. I'll put an engineering team and a test pilot on the job right away; in fact, I'll take personal charge myself. With luck, we can have your cycloplane ready for action in a few days."

"Swell, Dad! That's the main reason I called."

Tom brought his father up to date on certain details concerning the cybertron and the new engine mounts for his cycloplane. Then, after an exchange of affectionate family messages, the young inventor signed off.

Meanwhile, Chow had been packing a jungle kit for each man, which included water, food rations, and insect repellent. Doc Simpson loaded his own bag with medical instruments and extra first-aid gear in case of emergencies.

At the same time, each man was busy with scissors, needle, and packthread, fashioning himself a makeshift sleeping bag out of waterproof nylon fabric. Great rolls of the material were always carried aboard the *Sky Queen* for camouflage purposes.

Tom himself went to work at top speed in the ship's electronic laboratory. Assembling parts like a one-man production line, he constructed a small transistor-type walkie-talkie for every man, in case the group should become separated from one another.

The tropic sun was high overhead when the lunch-call clanging of Chow's triangle was heard over the ship's intercom. Hungrily the crew assembled for a tasty meal of ham sandwiches, salad, and lemonade.

"How soon do we hit the trail, skipper?" Slim asked as he got up from the table.

"In about an hour," Tom replied. "We'll all hit the sack for a short siesta first, so we can start out well rested."

Shortly before two o'clock, Tom roused the men from their naps. Shouldering their jungle kit bags, the rescue party lined up for the rugged overland trek.

Arv Hanson and two flight crewmen had been detailed to stay behind and guard the *Sky Queen*. Tom had equipped himself with a fairly strong radio transmitter to keep in constant touch with them.

"Remember, fellows," Tom warned his men, "we're in for some rough travel and the heat will be terrific until we reach higher ground. So take it easy until you get used to it."

With shouts of farewell from the three crewmen guarding the *Sky Queen,* the rescue party slogged forward into the jungle.

The undergrowth was so dense that almost at once the going became rugged. Swinging their machetes and hatchets, the men had to hack their way along, foot by foot and yard by yard.

On all sides, the towering forest rose about them—huge casuarina trees, oaks, palms, and pandanus. Dripping green moss festooned the branches and clung to the tree trunks.

Even the ground underfoot was soggy, covered with rotting vines and logs. "Like walkin' on a sponge!" Chow grumbled.

Every foot of the way, they were fascinated by strange sounds and splashes of brilliant color. Gaudy parrots and cockatoos screeched at them from the treetops. Other weird-looking birds with long plumage of orange, violet, or emerald green would occasionally flit into view.

"Birds of paradise," George Hedron explained. "Their feathers used to bring a fortune for decorating ladies' hats. In fact, the natives still use them for making plumed headdresses."

Once the trekkers sighted a comical-looking animal perched on a tree branch. It was snoozing contentedly with its head between the forepaws. At sight of Tom's rescue party, it arced to the ground in a prodigious leap and scuttled off through the undergrowth.

"And what might that be?" Chow demanded. "Sittin' Bull's nephew?"

Hedron chuckled. "Just a tree kangaroo!"

But the men were in no mood to enjoy the interesting surroundings. Streaming with perspiration and pestered by insects, every step seemed to add to their torture.

Turning to speak to Doc Simpson, Tom noticed a glazed look in Slim Davis's eyes.

"Slim! Are you all right?" he queried.

Tottering, Slim wiped the sweat from his brow. "Sure—just a bit bushed, I guess," he replied.

Suddenly Doc gasped and pointed to Red Jones. Apparently the redheaded crewman had not noticed that the rest of the group had halted. With drooping head and closed eyes, he stumbled forward.

"Catch him, someone!" Tom shouted.

But it was too late. Tripping over a tree root, Red sprawled headlong on the ground, then

At sight of Tom's rescue party, the startled
kangaroo scuttled off

groveled in the green foliage, too weak to rise. Doc Simpson and the others ran to his assist-

ance. "Heat prostration," the medico announced after a quick examination.

By bathing Red's forehead and holding smelling salts to the man's nose, Doc soon revived him. But Tom suggested that the group rest for a while.

While the men lounged, with their backs propped against tree trunks, the young inventor checked his pedometer.

"Wow! What a snail's pace!" he muttered.

"What's wrong, skipper?" Slim inquired.

"Since we left the *Sky Queen,* we're covered only about a mile in actual forward motion."

The depressing news was greeted with loud groans. To cool off from the steaming jungle heat, and to keep away the flies and mosquitoes, the men fanned themselves constantly.

In half an hour, the group resumed its trek. But again progress was slow. Gradually the jungle shadows deepened as the day drew to a close.

"Might be wise to stop soon and make camp," Hedron advised. "Night comes fast in this part of the world."

Tom agreed, but pointed out the importance of first finding a good campsite. Eventually the expedition halted near a shallow jungle stream.

While Chow made a fire and started preparing the evening meal, most of the men flopped down, completely exhausted.

Tom, however, decided to use what was left of daylight to scout around for enemies—human or animal.

"I'll go with you," Doc volunteered.

Keeping in close touch with each other, the two began ranging around the camp in widening circles. Suddenly a shout from Doc brought the scientist on the run.

"What is it?" yelled Tom, alert for danger.

In reply, Doc held up a waxy green plant with a small pink flower which he had just plucked from the ground. "A rare herb, used in certain drug preparations!" he explained. "Here's a whole patch of the stuff!"

With Tom's help, he began picking a supply to take back to Shopton for his medical experiments. Engrossed in their task, neither noticed that the ground was getting softer at every step.

Suddenly Tom realized they were both ankle-deep in the wet, spongy earth. Floundering for a foothold, he sank almost to the knees in oozy muck!

"Doc!" he cried. "It's a bog! We're getting sucked in!"

CHAPTER VIII

STONE-AGE ATTACK

IN A FRENZY of alarm, the two explorers tried to scramble back to firmer ground. But their efforts were futile—the treacherous bog only clutched them more securely in its slimy embrace. With every wallowing step, they plunged deeper and deeper into the morass.

"Hold it, Doc!" Tom gasped finally. "We're only making matters worse!"

Panting for breath, the two companions eyed each other in growing panic. They used their walkie-talkies to contact their friends, but there was no reply.

"Maybe if we yell, they'll hear us," Doc suggested.

They shouted themselves hoarse, but the only response was the mocking cries of jungle birds.

Tom said at last, "Doc, did you happen to pack any fishhooks in your jungle kit?"

The doctor stared in amazement. "No, but I have some large safety pins you could bend into hooks. Why?"

"Just an idea—which may not work. Give me

58

some pins and a reel of surgical thread, will you?"

By this time, both victims had sunk to their hips in the bubbling ooze. But Doc managed to get out the thread and pins and hand them to Tom. Working fast, the young scientist looped the thread through the ring on his jackknife to weight the line. Then he tied several of the bent pins to one end of the thread; the other end he tied to his belt.

Twirling the line around and around, he heaved it toward a clump of trees at the edge of the bog. After several misses, Tom finally succeeded in hooking a long trailing creeper which dangled from the tree branches.

Doc held his breath as Tom began gently reeling in the line. Both feared that under the strain, either the thread might break, or the pins be dislodged. Their last chance for survival would be lost! But finally the vine was close enough for Tom to reach out gingerly and grasp hold.

"You did it!" Doc exulted as Tom's hand finally reached out and grabbed the vine.

"Don't cheer until we make sure this is strong enough to support our weight," Tom warned him.

Doc told Tom to go first. "No sense overloading it," he said. "I'll hold this end."

Advancing along the creeper, hand over hand, Tom hauled himself slowly toward safe ground. Bathed in sweat and covered from head to foot with muck, he finally clawed and clambered his way out of the bog.

"Come on, Doc!" he called.

Minutes later, the physician collapsed in a heap alongside the young inventor.

"I owe you my life," he murmured gratefully.

Tom shook his head, grinning. "Without your surgical thread and those safety pins, we'd both have been out of luck."

After resting for a while, they headed back to camp. Step by step, the two young men groped their way by flashlight through the tangled jungle growth. But even with the yellow beams of their lights to guide them, the going was slow and tedious. Ten minutes later Tom stopped abruptly.

"What's the matter?" Doc inquired.

"We're going in circles!"

A sweep of his flashlight revealed the same patch of pink-flowered herbs which had lured them into the bog.

"Whew!" Doc shuddered and mopped his brow. "A few more steps and we might have walked right into that bog again!"

Heading once more toward camp, the two trekkers resumed their slow plodding through the jungle. Minutes went by. Still no flickering camp-fire greeted them through the trees.

Once again Tom stopped. "Let's face it, Doc," he said grimly, "we're lost."

"I suggest we shout some more," the physician suggested. "At least we may be within earshot by now."

"Okay—both barrels," Tom agreed. "And if there's no response, we'll try the walkie-talkie again."

Filling their lungs with air, the two companions let out a long-drawn bellow for help. A moment later the startled pair was cowering under a deadly hail of small, sharp-pointed stones!

"Take cover!" Tom yelled.

Shielding their faces, he and Doc plunged into the underbrush. For several minutes the stinging missiles continued to rain down all around them. Then the attack halted as abruptly as it had begun.

Crouching in the darkness, the two awaited another onslaught. But none came. Only the eerie night sounds of the jungle broke the silence.

"What do you make of that?" Doc whispered. "Unfriendly natives?"

"Must be."

Venturing out of their hiding place, they scouted around cautiously. None of their attackers was in sight.

Tom played his flashlight over the ground and kicked up several small polished stones the size of marbles. "Take a look at this ammunition. Those natives must have used slingshots."

Doc picked up one of the stones and examined it. "They weren't playing with peashooters, that's for sure! If one of these should hit a vital spot, it could kill a man!"

In spite of himself, Tom felt a chill of fear. "We'd better get back to camp pronto!" he advised.

Despite painful cuts and bruises, they pushed on through the jungle. Half an hour later they sighted Chow's campfire. A chorus of gasps and exclamations greeted them as they stumbled into the circle of firelight.

"Good night! What have you two been up to?" Slim demanded.

"You name it, we've had it," Tom said wearily as he sank to the ground.

Bruised, bloodstained, and covered with muck, he and Doc presented a startling appearance. As they washed in the nearby stream, they related the whole story. Then Doc painted their wounds with antiseptic.

"Now that you two mavericks are here," said Chow, "we sure ought to get at our grub. I'll dish out some stew." He turned away.

"Tom," said Red Jones, "what did the natives look like? I mean those guys who blasted you with stones."

Tom shrugged. "We didn't even catch a glimpse of them. They took us completely by surprise."

"Must be very primitive, though," Doc Simpson added. "Those missiles indicate a stone-age culture. Let's hope they're not cannibals to boot!"

"*Cannibals!*" Sam Barker turned pale at the thought. "Excuse me, but I think I've just lost my appetite!"

"Let's hope," said Slim, "that they have, too."

Chow winked at Tom, then frowned as if insulted. "Afore you go makin' any rash decisions, Sam, get a whiff o' this here mulligan I been concoctin' fer all you hungry trail hands."

Lifting the lid of his stewpot, the Texan stirred the savory, bubbling contents.

Sam sniffed the appetizing aroma. His face relaxed into a blissful grin. "Okay, Chow, you just convinced me. After all, a man's got to keep up his strength!"

With good-natured hoots and chuckles, the men gathered around the campfire and held out their plates to Chow. But underneath all the merriment ran a feeling of grim apprehension. Even though no one put it into words, the same thought was in every mind: *Had Bud and Hank fallen victim by now to a tribe of savage headhunters?*

Tom was especially worried. Many New Guinea tribesmen were reported friendly—at least on their first contact with white men. Did tonight's attack mean that the local natives had already suffered at the hands of hostile whites? If so, the rescue party could expect plenty of trouble!

To play safe, Tom assigned sentries to take turns standing watch throughout the night. He and Slim Davis took the first trick, then tumbled into their sleeping bags, stiff with exhaustion. Some time later Tom awoke to find Red Jones, who was on guard, shaking him urgently.

"Huh? Wh-what's up?" Tom mumbled sleepily, raising himself on one elbow.

"We just heard a shot, skipper!"

Instantly alert, Tom scrambled out of the sack. The jungle was shrouded in darkness.

For several minutes Tom and the two sentries waited tensely. But there were no further shots. Only the distant scream of a night bird broke the eerie stillness.

"Sure you weren't mistaken?" Tom asked.

The two sentries eyed each other uncertainly. "Well, it *sounded* like a shot," Red replied.

Tom stayed awake for another half hour. When nothing else happened, he finally went back to sleep, after first urging Red and his cowatcher to rouse him at the slightest hint of trouble.

Morning dawned without further incident. After breakfast, the expedition prepared to break camp.

Suddenly a startled screech from Sam Barker brought the whole rescue party running to his side. In speechless fright, he pointed to his sleeping bag.

Out slithered a sinister golden form with glittering green eyes!

CHAPTER IX

THE WINGED HORDE

"IT'S A PYTHON!" exclaimed George Hedron. "A green tree python!"

Inch by inch, the reptile squirmed its way out of Sam's sleeping bag.

"Looks more yaller to me than green," Chow muttered. "Not to mention all those black an' white speckles."

"This is a young one," Hedron explained. "As they get older, they turn a bright emerald green."

"Sam looks pretty green right now, himself!" someone guffawed.

Gulping hard and trembling visibly, Sam Barker looked sick indeed. "Y-y-you mean I've been c-c-curled up all night long with *that!*" he quavered.

Suddenly he sank down heavily in the jungle grass. "That settles it," he groaned. "I'm quitting this assignment right now!"

"Oh, no, you ain't, buckaroo!" said Chow firmly. Reaching out a gnarled but sinewy arm, Chow hauled the demoralized rescuer to his feet. "Now you listen here, Sam Barker. We got two

good friends, Bud and Hank, dependin' on us to
save their hides. An' brand my skillet, we ain't
goin' to let 'em down, even if it means stickin'
our own necks in the chopper! You savvy?"

Sam flushed under the cook's stern gaze and
seemed to take a fresh grip on himself. "I—I guess
you're right, Chow," he mumbled. "None of us
has any business quitting till we find Bud and
Hank."

"Now you're talkin'!" Beaming with approval,
the Texan clapped him on the back.

Meanwhile, the python had ceased moving,
even though it still hadn't emerged completely
from the sleeping bag. With unblinking beady
eyes, the snake stared sluggishly at the circle of
human beings.

"Looks as if it doesn't want to leave that nice
warm bed," observed Slim with a chuckle.

"Well, we're not taking it with us, that's for
sure," Tom announced.

Chopping off a long tree branch with his
machete, he cautiously prodded the reptile into
motion. As it slithered off through the underbrush, Hedron watched it disappear with a worried look.

"That little fellow may have some kin close
by," he warned the others. "And a full-grown
python is apt to be nasty. Keep a sharp lookout
when we hit the trail."

Later, while the rest of the party finished
stowing their gear, Tom began sending out a
signal.

"Rescue party calling *Sky Queen!* . . . Come in, please!"

In a few moments Arv Hanson's voice replied, "Hi, Tom! You just missed a message from Shopton."

"Anything important?" Tom inquired.

"Well, your dad's been called to Washington on a new defense contract. But he said he thinks that they have all the kinks ironed out of your cycloplane and the cybertron. In fact, the ship should be ready for test flying as soon as you get back."

"Swell news, Arv! Anything else?"

"Yes, the police have been talking with your cousin, Ed Longstreet, and now they're working on a tip from that curio dealer out in San Francisco. I didn't catch all the details, but apparently they know who has the stolen statue."

Tom gave a whoop of satisfaction. "Sounds as if things are really popping!" he remarked, then added dryly, "Been popping for us, too."

Briefly he related their adventures since leaving the *Sky Queen*. When he mentioned the mysterious gunshot which Red Jones and the other sentry had heard during the night, Arv broke in, "Hey! That must have been me, Tom!"

"You? How come?"

Arv explained that he had spotted moving lights in the jungle near the Flying Lab. "I figured it might be natives working up enough nerve to attack us, so I fired a shot in the air."

"What happened?"

"Nothing. The shot scared them off, I guess."

Tom mulled over the news thoughtfully. "Well, don't take any chances, Arv, but let's not start any feuds, either. If there *are* natives prowling around, I'd like to show them we come as friends, not enemies. The lives of Hank and Bud may depend on it!"

"You have a point there, skipper," Arv replied in a troubled voice. "From now on, I'll be careful."

After signing off, Tom hauled down his antenna and packed up the transmitter. Soon the rescue party was ready to hit the trail.

Again they were forced to hack their way through the dense jungle. But the early-morning freshness made the going pleasanter than before, and the shreds of mist still drifting among the trees lent a touch of nighttime coolness.

The men plodded along cheerfully, whistling or cracking jokes as they wielded their hatchets and machetes. At times they had to proceed single file. Eventually, however, the trees and underbrush thinned out into an open, rocky clearing.

"Hold it!" shouted Tom suddenly.

Crowding up behind him, the men gasped at the sight that met their eyes. A huge, glossy green serpent at least fourteen feet long lay stretched out on a flat-topped boulder.

"Wal, I'll be a knock-kneed bronc!" Chow whispered. "Reckon this here must be that varmint's kin we heard about!"

"That's right," George Hedron agreed.

Slowly coiling its tail, the python reared its head torpidly and stared at them through piercing eyes.

"Guess we interrupted its morning sun bath," Slim remarked.

"Either that or it needs a dose of vitamin-nies," Chow added. "Sure looks like a lazy critter!"

"No wonder. It's just eaten." Hedron pointed to a telltale bulge in the python's midsection.

"Oh, oh." Red Jones gulped nervously as he sized up the reptile's swallowing capacity. "Now what do you suppose it ate?"

"A baby wild pig, maybe," Hedron replied. "It's amazing what a python can digest."

"Well, don't look at me," Red protested. "And don't go giving that python any ideas, either!"

Always on the lookout for new delicacies, Chow began to mutter about "python pie," also mentioning his recipe for stewed rattlesnake. But Tom hastily vetoed the idea.

"Let this python enjoy its food, and we'll enjoy ours," the young inventor said, chuckling.

Giving the reptile a wide berth, the rescue party pressed forward. As the sun rose higher in the heavens, the heat became unbearable. Soon the men were dripping with sweat. To add to their discomfort, the stinging insects of the jungle seemed to be attracted by the glistening moisture on their skins.

"Am I just imagining things, or are these mosquitoes getting worse?" inquired Slim as he paused to slap his face and arms.

Tom brushed away several winged tormentors that were buzzing around his own head. "They sure—" With a gasp, he broke off. "Good night, fellows! Look behind us!"

Turning, the men gasped in horror. A dense cloud of mosquitoes, billowing out at least twenty yards in width, was bearing down on them through the trees!

"Sufferin' horned toads, a whole army of 'em!" yelled Chow. "Let's get goin'!"

"Quick! Break out your insect repellent!" Doc ordered as they scampered for safety.

Clawing into their kits, the crewmen pulled

To escape the cloud of mosquitoes,

out tubes of ointment and began rubbing the salve on their faces, legs, and arms. But the vicious gnats came swarming around them before the job was half done.

"It's not working!" groaned Red.

"Nothing would help with a swarm this thick!" mumbled Hedron, flailing both arms in an effort to drive off the attackers.

Relentlessly the mosquitoes closed in on their victims, deafening them with a constant shrill buzzing. Every square inch of exposed skin seemed to be covered with clusters of the tiny brutes.

In desperation, the men broke into a wild run,

Tom and Chow plunged into the stream

scattering in all directions through the trees. Still the winged tormentors pursued them!

Tom found himself tearing along side by side with Chow, who displayed amazing speed for his portly size and bowlegs.

"Ain't that water I see up ahead?" panted the Texan, pointing to a ribbon of silver sparkling among the trees.

"It's a stream, all right," gasped Tom. Raising his voice, he yelled, "This way, all of you! We can throw off the insects by ducking under water!"

Reaching the bank of the stream, he and Chow plunged headfirst into the gleaming depths.

CHAPTER X

CHOW SEES A GHOST

THOUGH ITS SURFACE glinted in the sun, the water proved to be stagnant and murky. Once submerged, Tom and Chow found themselves groping among a tangle of weeds and oozing mud. When they finally surfaced, the deadly mosquitoes were still humming and swarming in all directions.

"Keep down, except for your mouth and nose!" Tom shouted, hoping there were no crocodiles lurking about.

The cook needed no urging to obey orders. Flapping his arms and treading water desperately, he tilted his head far back and managed to stay almost completely under water.

Gradually the cloud of insects passed over.

"Okay, I guess it's safe now," Tom announced, popping his head up. With a few swift strokes, he swam back to shore.

Spluttering, Chow followed him. Together,

73

they clambered out onto the bank of the stream, Tom lending the cook a helping hand. Both were coated with a mixture of mud and green scum.

The stout old Texan was so exhausted that he lay heaving and panting for several minutes before he found his voice. Then he muttered weakly:

"I don't know which is worse—drownin' in that mud puddle, or gettin' et up alive by them flyin' buzz saws!"

"I'll take the puddle any day!" Tom chuckled. A moment later he sat up sharply. "Hey! Where are the others?"

Chow opened his eyes and peered around. "They ain't in sight. Reckon they musta ducked for cover somewheres else, when you an' me jumped in the drink—if you call that stuff fit fer drinkin'!"

Tom reached in to his kit and pulled out his compact walkie-talkie, thankful that he had sealed the unit in a watertight case. After hoisting the antenna, he thumbed the signal button several times and spoke into the mike:

"Tom calling all hands! . . . Tom calling all hands! . . . Report, please!"

First one voice, then another, filtered back over the receiver. "This is Slim, Tom!" . . . "Sam Barker reporting, skipper!". . . "Doc here, Tom!"

In a few minutes every man was contacted. "We'll regroup as soon as possible at the spot where we scattered," the young inventor told them.

It was a sorry-looking band of rescuers who assembled on the trail a short time later. Every man was covered with insect bites. Red Jones— the worst bitten of the group—was puffy-faced from the savage attack.

Tom led the men to the jungle stream so they could bathe their tortured, itching skin. Then Doc Simpson swabbed each one with a soothing lotion to reduce the swelling and relieve the irritation.

"Guess we might as well have lunch before we push on," Tom decided.

Chow boiled some water and brewed tea, while the men nibbled on cold rations. After a short siesta, the group started off again.

Progress became slower as they plodded upward through the foothills ringing the valley. At some points, the trees and luxuriant green foliage were not so dense as before. But this helped the men little. The steep climb was more exhausting than hacking their way on level ground.

By midafternoon they reached a narrow, rocky defile. Stringing out into single file, they threaded their way through the pass with Tom in the lead.

As they emerged on the other side, the young inventor passed the word to take a rest. One by one, the men threw themselves on the ground, breathing hard from exertion.

"Where's Hedron?" Tom inquired, when the zoologist failed to appear. Supposedly, he had been bringing up the rear. But none of the other men knew what had happened to him.

Tom peered back through the gorge. There was no sign of movement among the rocks or shrubbery. "Hey, George!" he yelled, cupping his hands. *"George Hedron!"*

His voice echoed and re-echoed between the high-walled cliffs, startling a flock of red and yellow jungle birds into screaming flight. But the shouts brought no response from the zoologist.

Thoroughly alarmed, Tom beamed out a call over his walkie-talkie. Again he received no answer.

"Maybe those high cliffs are blocking the signal," Slim Davis suggested.

"Could be." With a worried frown, Tom ran his fingers through his blond crew cut. "Anyhow, we've got to find him. He may be hurt!"

Ordering his men to regroup, Tom led them back through the pass. On the other side, he called again over his walkie-talkie. Still no reply.

"We'd better fan out and look for him," Tom told the others. "And be sure to keep in touch by walkie-talkie—we don't want another man missing!"

Leaving the beaten trail which the rescue party had carved through the wilderness, Tom struck off into the underbrush. Trailing vines and creepers mingled on all sides with gorgeous orchids in colors of gold, purple, crimson, and orange.

Suddenly a glint of sunlight caught his eye. Peering into the distance, Tom saw a silver wire spearing up through the trees. At the very instant he saw it, the wire began to disappear from view. It was a walkie-talkie antenna being lowered!

With a shout, Tom crashed forward through the tangled green foliage. A moment later he emerged into a tiny clearing. There stood Hedron, smiling happily. Beside him huddled a weird, brownish-gray animal, strapped in a bag of wire netting.

"Good night, where have you been?" Tom demanded.

"Capturing a padmelon." Hedron pointed to his prize. Looking somewhat like a huge rat, the padmelon was almost three feet long. "It's really a species of kangaroo," Hedron went on. "The females have a pouch, and—"

"That's all very interesting," Tom interrupted curtly, "but why the dickens didn't you let us know what you were up to? Don't you realize the whole rescue party is searching for you?"

"I'm sorry," Hedron apologized. "I spotted this padmelon burrowing through the underbrush, and it seemed like too good a chance to miss. I couldn't call you or make any kind of a signal for fear of scaring the thing away."

Tom was greatly annoyed. Hedron apparently thought it more important to capture the ratlike marsupial than to rescue Bud and Hank. But Tom held his temper and said calmly:

"Well, now that you've trapped it, what do you propose to do? I still wouldn't have found you if I hadn't spotted your aerial."

"I tried to contact you just now," Hedron explained, "but my walkie-talkie doesn't seem to be working. I guess it *was* pretty foolish to wander off like this," he added lamely. "If you hadn't happened to find me, I might have wound up in a real jam!"

Somewhat mollified, Tom examined Hedron's walkie-talkie and soon located the trouble—a disconnected wire, probably jarred loose while Hedron was chasing the padmelon. After fixing it, he called his men together and the trek was resumed.

At dusk the exhausted group made camp near a shallow, cavelike opening in the mountainside. Chow tried to tempt everyone's appetite with a tasty meal of hot rice and canned meat loaf. But the men were too sore from insect bites and tired to enjoy it. They ate in silence, then sprawled out to doze.

At last Tom and Chow were the only ones still awake. While the cook cleared away the supper remains, Tom propped himself against a big rock and stared up into space. Above the clustering treetops, the night sky was brilliant with stars.

Idly, the young inventor picked out the Southern Cross and other tropic constellations. As he thought of Bud and Hank, a lump formed in his throat. By now, their plight must be desperate. Perhaps they were already dead!

Worst of all, Tom and his rescue party were helpless to aid them. All they could do was plod along, mile by mile, through the jungle at a snail's pace. Meanwhile, there were Arv and the two crewmen to worry about, as well. What if hostile natives should launch another attack on the *Sky Queen?*

"Yi-i-eee!" Without warning, a shriek of terror split the air!

Jumping up in alarm, Tom saw Chow bounding toward him. Popeyed with fright, the cook stumbled over the embers of the campfire and would have sprawled headlong if Tom hadn't caught him.

"Chow! What's the matter?" the young scientist demanded.

"A g-g-ghost! I jest seen a ghost!" yelled the terrified Texan.

CHAPTER XI

MYSTERIOUS MISSILES

"NOW CALM DOWN, Chow, and talk sense!"
Tom advised the cook. "What is it you saw?"

"Two horrible big eyes—starin' at me out o'
the darkness!" Chow replied. "It's a jungle ghost,
I tell you, or I'd 'a' shot it."

"All right, all right!" said Tom. The cowpoke
was trembling like a nervous bronc. "Just show
me where you saw this, Chow."

"Over yonder at the other end o' camp."

With Chow, Tom ran to the spot where the
cook had been cleaning the mess gear.

"There they are!" Chow stabbed the darkness
with a quivering forefinger. "Look at 'em! Starin'
at us jest like a couple o' burnin' coals!"

Ahead, beyond the glow of the campfire, two
huge reddish eyes peered out of the night. By
this time the whole rescue party was awake and
on its feet. Gaping with half-sleepy amazement,
they stared back at the weird immovable eyes.

Tom suddenly chuckled and threw an arm

around the Texan. "Relax, Chow. I'm sure it's only some New Guinea bird or animal. Let's flash a light on it."

One of the men hastily procured a flashlight and aimed its beam into the darkness. The light revealed a queer-looking animal perched on a tree branch. With its domelike skull, huge ruby eyes, and a tail partly furred, partly smooth-skinned, it looked like a little gremlin.

"Why, it's a cuscus!" exclaimed George Hedron.

"I don't care *what* kind of ornery cuss it is!" Chow retorted, but he colored a little shame-facedly. "It ain't got no business scarin' civilized folks half to death!"

The cook stalked forward toward the tree branch and made shooing motions with his apron. "G'wan now! Clear out before I take the skillet to you!"

The cuscus, instead of darting off in panic, continued to stare at Chow with the same blank expression. Somewhat unnerved, the Westerner turned to George Hedron.

"D-don't jest stand there!" he cried. "Get that blasted critter out o' here!"

Hedron shook his head. "Not me. This creature is slow-moving and slow-witted, but it has a *very* nasty temper when aroused."

At that moment the cuscus bristled as if about to attack and let out a shrill cry of *"Chit-chit-chit!"*

Chow was so startled that he almost fell over

backward. Retreating hastily, he muttered, "New Guinea varmint!" The other men shook with laughter.

As if satisfied that it had won a victory, the cuscus finally scuttled off into the darkness. Chow heaved a sigh of relief.

"I'd better assign guards for the night," said Tom. "We'll take turns in pairs. Red and Sam, suppose you take the first watch."

The rest of the party stretched out in their sleeping bags around the cave entrance. Soon the camp was wrapped in silence.

Just before dawn broke, the group was rudely awakened by a wild *whooshing* sound overhead.

"Bats!" yelled Slim, who was one of the sentries on watch. "There's a million of 'em!"

The air was black with the hideous creatures. Even at a distance their wing span seemed enormous—as wide as a man's outstretched arms!

Awakening in alarm, the men scrambled from their sleeping bags and jumped to their feet.

"Flying foxes, aren't they?" Tom asked Hedron.

The zoologist nodded, staring in fascination at the oncoming horde. "That's what most people call them. Actually they're a species of fruit bat."

The next moment, the rescue party began to scatter in panic. Instead of passing over, the bats zoomed straight at them!

"Oh—oh! This cave must be their home!" Tom exclaimed.

The words were hardly out of his mouth when one of the creatures swooped past, grazing Tom's cheek with its wing tip. The young scientist re-coiled. But the bat banked, and circled around. Before Tom could dodge, he was whacked so hard on the face that he fell flat!

The other men had taken refuge behind trees, but now dived to the ground. In three minutes the raid was over. The bats disappeared com-pletely inside the cavern's inky interior.

"That cave must be very deep," observed Doc.

Chow muttered, "I ain't takin' any chances. If you all want grub, you got to follow me to a safe distance to get it."

But when daylight filtered down through the trees the cook changed his mind. While the men splashed their faces in the water of a nearby creek, he built a fire and started breakfast.

Hedron came up to Tom. "I think I'll go out and scout around for some wallaby tracks," he said. "Like to capture one if I can."

"Don't you think your padmelon's enough of a load to haul with us?" Tom remarked.

Hedron shrugged and smiled vaguely. "Oh, I'll turn that loose as soon as I make a few more notes and pictures." Shouldering his kit, the zoologist wandered off.

Soon the appetizing aroma of bacon and corn meal filled the air. A few minutes later Chow sounded the breakfast gong by banging on his stew kettle.

"Okay, buckaroos! Eat hearty!" he urged. "Goin' to need all your strength to beat through this jungle an' find Bud an'—"

His words ended in a yelp of pain as a hail of sharp-pointed stones suddenly spattered the camp.

"It's another attack!" Tom yelled. "Run for cover, everybody!"

Openmouthed with dismay, the men wavered a moment in confusion as another volley of missiles shot out of the jungle. Tom's group started for the shallow cave opening but changed their minds. The bats might try another assault!

"This way!" Tom shouted. Hugging the mountainside, he scrambled upward among the rocks and boulders to where he had glimpsed another cave.

The men bumped into one another in their haste to follow. Once inside the cave, they huddled together in the darkness, panting.

"Wow!" gasped Slim. "Tom, it looks as if your old pals haven't forgotten us."

"They've probably been keeping tabs on us right along," the young inventor muttered.

Tensely he waited, wondering if the attackers might close in for a fight to the finish. But apparently they were being cagey, either out of fear or caution. Ten minutes ticked by without any further sign of the enemy.

"Stay here," Tom ordered the others. "I'll take a peek outside."

He disappeared but returned in a few moments with news that no one had bothered him. "I'm pretty sure that our attackers have gone," he added. Then Tom frowned. "I'm worried about Hedron. No sign of him."

Emerging from the cave, the men descended the hill and fanned out cautiously around the camp. But they found no trace of their attackers or of the biologist either. As Doc Simpson started to attend the men who had received cuts from the missiles, a cheery voice asked:

"Hey, what's going on?"

The group swung around to see George Hedron sauntering casually toward them among the trees.

"A range war, that's what!" growled Chow. "Lucky you didn't get yer scalp lifted out there, son!"

He explained what had happened. Hedron was amazed.

"And to think," he remarked ruefully, "while you guys were having all that excitement, I couldn't even scare up a field mouse, much less a wallaby!"

Though Tom wanted to push on in his search for Bud and Hank, he delayed long enough for a newly cooked breakfast to be prepared. Meanwhile, he examined some of the stone missiles.

"Find something, skipper?" Doc Simpson inquired, noticing the other's excited look.

"I sure have!" Tom exclaimed. "These stones are made of holmium, like the statue that was stolen back in Shopton!"

The news aroused a flurry of interest. The men clustered around, agog at Tom's discovery.

"You're sure?" Hedron demanded.

"As sure as I can be without a spectrographic

analysis." Pointing to the shimmering yellow-orange pellets, Tom explained how their color, texture, weight, hardness, and general "feel" were exactly like that of the animal figurine.

"Great Scott!" put in Doc. "That means there must be a supply of rare earths around here somewhere!"

"Right! And that's not all," Tom went on. "Remember that message Arv Hanson picked up from Bud or Hank? It contained the words: *'rare . . . like what you—'* Well, the whole phrase might have been *'rare earths, like what you found in the statue!'* "

As the men burst into excited comments, Tom's mind whirled with interesting possibilities. Could it be that his lost friends had discovered the secret of how the missiles were made? Surely the ore had not been mined and processed by stone-age savages!

But how old were the missiles? Did they date back to prehistoric times? *Or had they been fashioned by living enemies!*

CHAPTER XII

THE SLINGSHOT CLUE

"WELL, what do we do now, skipper?" asked Red Jones, breaking in on Tom's thoughts.

"You fellows eat your breakfast," the young inventor replied. "Slim and Doc, how about you two coming with me?"

"Sure," Slim agreed promptly. "But what's up?"

"An idea just occurred to me. If we can track those men who attacked us, they *might* lead us to Bud and Hank."

"By George, you're right, Tom!" Doc Simpson was enthusiastic. "Let's go!"

Circling back and forth around the camp, the trio studied the damp soil and thick green underbrush for signs of human footprints. Unfortunately, Tom's own men had trampled much of the ground just a few minutes before, while searching for their unseen enemies.

"We'll have to go farther," said Slim.

But even beyond the fringes of camp in the

direction from which the missiles had come, they could detect no footprints or tracks of any kind.

"Looks as if we're out of luck." Doc sighed as he paused to mop his brow.

Tom nodded, scowling with disappointment. "These jungle natives are past masters at covering their tracks. I guess we're out of our league when we try to solve—"

Tom broke off. Reaching into the tall grass, he scooped up a long strip of untanned leather. It was tapered at both ends, and broadened at the middle into a sort of pouch.

"What is it?" Slim demanded, with a puzzled expression.

"A thong slingshot—the same kind David used on Goliath. And probably what they used on us just now, too."

"No doubt about it," Doc agreed. "At least we're on the right track!"

With renewed energy the trio continued their search. None of them, however, could find any other clues or trail signs. After an hour they finally gave up and returned to camp.

Chow cooked a fresh batch of food for them. While they ate, the other men examined the thong slingshot and discussed the mysterious unseen natives.

"Reckon we'd better keep our eyes peeled right sharp from now on," the Texas cook commented. "Jest like pioneers passin' through Injun country. If we don't, we're apt to wind up missin' our hair, or even our heads!"

"You're right, Chow." Tom nodded. "From now on, it'll be every man's job to keep a lookout while we're on the move. And no stragglers!" he added, with a glance at George Hedron.

The zoologist made no comment, but when the rescue party hit the trail, he was ready. Again the route led upward through the highlands, with towering purple mountain ranges soaring into the clouds in the distance.

Then the ground seemed to flatten out into a plateau. But the terrain was as rugged as ever, and the tangled vegetation even thicker and more impassable as they pushed on. Dirty, footsore, bathed in sweat, the men groaned and grunted with the effort as they hacked their way forward with ax and machete.

"I sure wish I was back on the open range," Chow burst out. "Out there a hombre can see where he's headin'."

Tom's heart sank as he thought of the distance that still remained between where they were and the crashed plane. At this snail's pace, how could they possibly reach Bud and Hank?

"Maybe I'd be wiser to go back to Shopton, bring the cycloplane here, and try taking it down through the storm area between the volcanoes," he thought, "instead of continuing this trek."

Again and again, Tom turned the problem over in his mind as he trudged on, leading his group almost automatically. But suddenly a cry from Slim Davis shocked Tom out of his reverie.

"Sam! Your legs!" Glancing toward Barker, the

young inventor gasped to find that the man's skin below the knees was covered with blood!

"Land leeches!" Tom exclaimed.

"Good night! We've all got 'em!" Slim cried out.

The others examined their own limbs. Then, dropping their knives and axes, they began clawing at their legs, plucking off the stubborn bloodsuckers as fast as their fingers would permit.

Doc Simpson brought out his first-aid gear and smeared a soothing salve over everyone's legs. "That'll help to stop the bleeding," he explained. "Now take some of this gauze, wind it around your legs and ankles, and tape it on. That'll discourage the leeches."

In a few minutes the group was ready to continue. As they pushed on, Sam Barker sang out:

"Ah, come to beautiful New Guinea!
Vacation spot of the world!
This island paradise—"

"—is a right good place to go loco!" Chow finished sourly.

The others laughed and began hacking their way again. Just before noon they reached a deep chasm, spanned by a swaying, rickety bridge made of vines apparently woven together by the natives.

"Only way to get across," Slim commented. "Look below!"

The ravine, sheering downward a hundred feet or more, seemed deep enough to hold a tall building. Below lay a tangled mass of trees and vegeta-

With a creaking screech, the bridge fell into the chasm

tion so thickly matted and intertwined that it seemed to form a continuous green carpet across the floor of the gulch.

"What now, Tom?" Slim Davis asked.

"I'll go first and test the bridge."

There was an instant outcry. "No, don't do that, skipper!" Red Jones exclaimed. "That thing's not safe."

Chow put in, "If anyone goes, it'd better be ole Chow here. Reckon if that bridge'll hold me, it'll hold anyone!"

But Tom brushed aside their protests. "I got you fellows to come on this expedition," he pointed out quietly, "and I don't expect any of you to take a risk *I* wouldn't take. Besides, these natives are clever at vine weaving. Here goes!"

Advancing step by step, he proceeded cautiously onto the narrow span. The men held their breaths. The bridge bounced and swayed dizzily over the yawning gulf.

"I don't like this here business," Chow said worriedly.

"Nor I," added Sam Barker.

Tom was almost at the halfway point, when Doc Simpson, who was watching his progress through field glasses, gave a yell of alarm. "The anchor ropes on the far side are giving way!" he screamed.

The vines were now held by only a few strands!

Tom had halted at the doctor's cry and looked back. His frantic friends were signaling with their arms for him to return. A chorus of voices broke into agonized shouts:

"Come back! Come back!"

Uncertain, Tom hesitated for an instant. Then, looking ahead, he saw what was happening and turned to dash back to safety.

He was too late. With a creaking *screech*, the far end of the bridge gave way. Tom plunged toward the bottom of the chasm!

CHAPTER XIII

AN OMINOUS MESSAGE

TOM'S companions watched in horror as the broken bridge arced across the chasm. The sickening plunge had caught Tom unawares, but he had miraculously managed to grab the braided strands of the vine bridge and hook his arms and legs through them.

As the dangling bridge hit the near wall of the rocky ravine, the smashing impact knocked the breath out of Tom. While he swung perilously, everything swimming before his eyes, his friends swarmed into action.

"Grab those vines!" shouted Slim, taking charge. "Hoist! But gently!"

Hauling on the upper end of the bridge, the men raised Tom inch by inch. Despite the men's careful hoisting, he was bumped and scraped against the cliff face. When he finally was eased over the edge, he was only half-conscious. Quickly the others freed him from the tangled strands and laid him on soft grass. Doc went to work with smelling salts, but it was several moments before

Tom could speak. Then he grinned up wanly at the circle of faces. "Didn't know I was a trapeze artist, did you?"

"Brand my stabilizer, I thought you was a *ex*-trapeze artist fer a while there!" gulped Chow. "Now stay put, son!" he added hastily, as the young scientist tried to get up.

Tom obeyed orders meekly, while Doc painted his cuts and abrasions with antiseptic.

A moment later Slim came rushing up, an alarmed look on his face. "That was no accident, skipper! Those bridge ropes were cut almost clean through!"

There was a moment of uneasy silence, then Doc asked, "Who do you suppose did it? Those same natives who gave us the stone treatment?"

Tom scowled worriedly. "It seems as if someone is determined to keep us from reaching Bud and Hank."

"And maybe this time they succeeded," put in Hedron. He gestured across the chasm. "What do we do now—fly over?"

The searchers were in a tough spot. The ravine was not only deep, but in both directions it extended far into the jungle.

Chow scratched his bristly chin. "Wal, it'd sure take too long to walk around, so I reckon that means we gotta climb all the way down an' then up t'other side."

"Oh, brother!" groaned Red Jones. "Another day, maybe two, lost!"

The same thought was passing through Tom's

mind. "Look, fellows," he said, "Bud's and Hank's lives may depend on us reaching them as soon as possible. Slim, could you take over if I left?"

"Sure. But why?"

"There's a chance that I can make the descent between the volcanoes in the cycloplane."

"But that's way back in Shopton," Sam Barker interrupted.

"I know," Tom said, "but now that we've cleared a trail, I should be able to get back to the *Sky Queen* pretty fast. I could fly home to the plant in ten hours, test the cycloplane, and be back here in New Guinea in two or three days." He smiled enthusiastically. "The way things look now, I might be able to reach the scene of the crash sooner than you fellows."

The men looked at one another, then agreed that the young inventor was probably right.

Chow offered the only protest. "Brand my coyote steak, you ain't makin' that trip through the jungle alone, son—not with all them stone-slingin' head-hunters around. I'm goin' back with you!"

Tom agreed to let him go along. All through the afternoon the two traveled at a fast pace. At dusk they halted for a cold snack, then continued their trek. Night came on, cloaking the jungle in inky darkness. Tom and Chow pulled out flashlights.

"We'd better keep the beams close to the ground," Tom advised, "so we won't attract attention."

The yellow cones of light scooped a path forward over the matted vegetation. But Chow's beam began to grow dim. Finally it flickered out altogether.

The loss of light was a serious handicap. With only one beam to guide them, their speed was cut down. They picked their way along, inch by inch, to avoid tripping over exposed tree roots and tangled underbrush.

Finally Tom called a halt. "I guess we'd better stay here and try to get some rest between now and daylight."

Easing off their heavy kits, they propped themselves up against the bole of a giant casuarina tree. Tom decided to contact the *Sky Queen* and notify Arv Hanson of his plans.

"Here, I'll do it," Chow offered. "Got my walkie-talkie right here, all handy-like." As he groped in the dark for the sender, the cook continued, "Brand my radarscope, I'll sure be glad to get back to civil-*i*-za-shun where a man—"

He broke off as a strange voice suddenly spoke crisply out of the walkie-talkie. *"The charge is working to perfection. We're ready for the capture."* Then there was silence.

"Jumpin' Jehosaphat! Who was that?" gasped Chow, realizing he had turned on the listening device.

"I wish I knew!" Tom replied, as a surge of impending danger swept over him. "That certainly was no native's voice. And those words had a sinister ring."

Apparently there were other English-speaking persons within a short range, using the same radio frequency. And, judging from the message, they were engaged in some unsavory plot. By this time, perhaps, they knew all about his rescue plans, Tom decided.

"Chow, we have no time to lose! I don't know what's going on here, but the sooner we get back with that cycloplane, the happier I'll be!"

Under the circumstances, it seemed best not to communicate with the *Sky Queen*. Chow left the set on for incoming messages but none came. The mystery went unsolved.

At the first streak of daylight, Tom and Chow again set off. Without bothering to eat, they shouldered their kits and plunged forward at a steady jog trot. In two hours they reached the forest clearing where the great silver-winged jet plane stood.

"Thank goodness it's still here in one piece," Tom reflected.

Arv Hanson and his two crewmen came crowding to the open hatch to greet Tom and Chow.

"Something wrong?" demanded Arv, fearful of bad news. After Tom reported the events of the past twenty-four hours, Hanson said, "We've had a rough go of it ourselves."

"Another attack?"

"Last night. This time they came right up to the ship and let go with a hail of stones. Luckily there was no damage."

While Tom explained his plans, Chow hurried to the ship's galley and prepared a hasty breakfast.

"Sure feels good to be back in my lil ole flyin' chuck wagon!" he told the others as he served porridge, bacon, waffles, and cocoa.

"Well, don't think we're not glad to *have* you back." Bill Bennings, one of the flight crewmen, chuckled as he finished his third waffle.

Breakfast over, Arv Hanson remarked to the cook, "If Tom can spare you on his trip home, how'd you like to stay behind here with me?"

The Texan asked in surprise, "Why?"

Arv explained a plan which had been taking shape in his mind. "These natives must be lurking close by. If they thought all of us had gone, they might come out in the open. Then you and I, Chow, could find out what they're up to."

Chow glanced at Tom to see what he thought of the plan.

"It's a good idea," said the young inventor. "If you did find out what their game is, you could warn Slim and the others." Suddenly Tom snapped his fingers. "Say, we might even be able to *trick* those enemies into showing themselves!"

"How?" asked Arv.

"By leaving some bait—a walkie-talkie for instance."

Arv grinned. "That ought to bring them out!"

After readying the *Sky Queen* for take-off, the five men sauntered casually among the trees, as though stretching their legs. Tom returned first. In a careless, offhand manner he laid an extra walkie-talkie, minus vital parts, on the ground.

Tom now busied himself under the fuselage,

supposedly making a last-minute inspection. Finally he climbed aboard the plane, ignoring the walkie-talkie as if he had forgotten it.

A few minutes later Bill Bennings and the other flight crewman returned. They too crawled aboard through the main hatch.

Soon the ground shook with a mighty roar, as Tom gunned the engines of the jet lifters. The *Sky Queen* soared aloft and disappeared.

Once again, the sounds of the surrounding jungle became normal. The gaudy cockatoos and other tropical birds which had been scared away by the Flying Lab's take-off came cawing and screaming back to their regular roosts.

Meanwhile, Arv and Chow were perched in the branches of a tree. Well-hidden by the thick green foliage, they waited uncomfortably.

Suddenly Arv whispered with a look of excitement:

"Someone's coming!"

CHAPTER XIV

STORM TEST

FREEZING into silence, Arv and Chow waited tensely in their tree perch to see who was coming. Two dark-skinned natives stepped into the clearing.

Tall and muscular, they were naked except for a loincloth in front, with a sort of bustle in back made out of a cluster of leaves. Their hair was thick and woolly, and their noses were pierced with long, curved slivers of shell. Slowly and cautiously, they approached the walkie-talkie bait on the ground.

"Reckon they think it's goin' to bite!" whispered Chow.

At last one of the men worked up enough courage to touch the object. When nothing happened, he grabbed it and the two trotted off into the jungle.

"Let's follow 'em!" Arv urged, sliding down the trunk.

Making as little noise as possible, he and Chow

hurried after the natives. At first it was easy to detect the bent grasses and foliage which marked their trail. But suddenly both trail and natives vanished.

Chow took off his hat and scratched his head. "I used to be purty good at cuttin' sign a bunch o' strays, but I sure can't savvy these hombres!"

Gloomy over the failure of their plan, he and Arv trudged back to the clearing.

"At least we ought to warn Slim and the others by radio," said Arv. "But I'd hate to have the message picked up."

Chow brooded in silence a few moments, then brightened. "Say! Mebbe we could talk in code— like, fer instance:

> *One, two, buckle my shoe!*
> *We smell somethin' fishy,*
> *An' it ain't lobster stew!"*

Arv chuckled. "It's worth trying. And we'll keep our promise to Tom."

Meanwhile, the *Sky Queen* was streaking northeastward across the Pacific. Tom spurred the ship to terrific speed. While it was on automatic pilot, the crew, Bill Bennings and Herb Shawk, took over and Tom caught some sleep.

Day and night were telescoped as the group crossed the successive time zones. They circled in for a landing above the Enterprises airstrip at eight o'clock in the morning.

Tom had radioed ahead to George Dilling. As a result, Tom's whole family and Phyl Newton were on hand to greet him. There was an exchange of kisses and handshakes, then a quick briefing on the rescue party's efforts to find Bud and Hank.

"N-no sign of them?" Sandy bit her lip to keep back the tears.

"I'm sure they're alive," Tom said, putting an arm around her. "And now, one hour at the house, then I must test the cycloplane."

A relaxing shower, clean clothes, and a hot home-cooked breakfast gave Tom new energy. Hopping into his sports car, he drove back to Swift Enterprises. Here he spent several hours personally going over his cycloplane. After checking the cybertron, the ultrasonic generator, and the new engine mounts, Tom felt sure that the ship was completely ready for its final test.

"Well I'm off, Dad," he said. "And by the way, will you call Ed Longstreet and ask him if he'd go back to New Guinea with me? I may need help in talking to the natives if I run into any of them."

"I'll phone him right away, son."

Tom donned his flying suit and climbed into the cockpit of the cycloplane. Bob Jeffers, the crew chief, gave him thumbs up.

Signaling back, Tom switched on the power. As the spinning drums hummed into action, the plane soared skyward to twenty thousand feet.

"So far so good," the young pilot muttered to himself. "Now for the acid test."

With a steady hand, he opened the jet throttle. Keeping his eyes glued to the air-speed indicator, he watched the needle creep around the dial . . . *350 knots . . . 400 . . . 450 . . . 500 . . .*

Tom gave a whoop of joy—the ship had passed the crucial speed range without a tremor!

"But I still haven't taken her through the sound barrier," he reflected cautiously.

He zoomed upward in a steep climb, then leveled off at fifty thousand feet.

A voice from the tower cut in, "How does she handle, skipper?"

"Terrific so far," Tom replied. "Tell you more in a minute or so. I'm going to dive."

"Okay. I'll listen for the boom."

"You won't hear it, Mac. I'll shoot the works over Lake Carlopa, so as not to disturb anybody."

A moment later Tom went into a 60-degree dive—the nose-over floating him slightly off his seat. Below, the broad blue patch of lake water settled squarely into his line of sight. Then, suddenly, he was boring down at dizzy, screaming speed. In less than sixty seconds he could be plunging into the lake!

Calmly Tom watched the air-speed indicator wind up. A white needle was creeping clockwise, as a red-and-yellow striped one moved counterclockwise.

Suddenly the needles crossed Mach 1! He was through the sound barrier!

The cycloplane was roaring downward at almost 900 knots when Tom finally pulled out of the dive. For a moment the G-force glued him to his seat. Then his body relaxed as he leveled off.

Grinning happily, Tom put the ship through a punishing series of aerobatics—rolls, steep turns, and loops. Not once did the cycloplane show the faintest sign of bucking or loss of control!

"Well, are you still with us?" came the voice from the tower.

Tom chuckled. "Mac, she's smooth as silk—really out of this world!"

A splotch on his radar screen indicated a storm somewhere off to the east, probably over the ocean. Eager to test his new craft still further, Tom sped toward the disturbance. The skies darkened and the sea below foamed and crested into huge, mountainous waves.

"Wow! Looks like a real blow!" he observed with satisfaction.

Soon he was streaking into the thick of the storm. A vivid flash of lightning split the sky, followed by a boom of thunder. Winds of near-hurricane velocity battered against the canopy. But through it all the cycloplane soared and swooped smoothly.

Switching on the cybertron, Tom relaxed in his seat. Without a tremor, the automatic brain took over control of the ship. The gyrostabilizer controlling the rotation of the cylinders kept the plane on an even keel.

"Talk about floating on a cloud!" Tom chuckled.

Suddenly a warning bell and flash of light drew

his attention to the scope. Some unknown object was plummeting down directly above him! The cybertron eased the ship neatly out of the way.

To Tom's amazement, the object proved to be a parachuting pilot!

Grabbing the controls, Tom banked and circled in a tight turn. Then he slowed the drums, causing the cycloplane to drop steeply.

Maneuvering under the parachutist, Tom slid open the canopy. A moment later the flier was cutting his shroud lines and easing himself safely inside the rescue craft.

"Thanks a million!" he gasped. "But what in the name of Jupiter is this plane—a flying saucer?"

Tom laughed. "I call it a cycloplane."

"But what holds it up?"

Tom explained briefly, adding, "Like to try it?"

The stranger took over the controls. "Why, it's the steadiest thing I've ever flown!" he exclaimed. "This crate's got everything! It's safer than a trainer and hotter than a pistol! You say it'll cruise on land, too?"

When Tom nodded with a grin, the stranger went on, "By the way, I'm Lieutenant Deever, Naval Reserve. My jet lost a wing when I pulled out of a dive. I'd have wound up in the drink if it hadn't been for you!"

"Glad I happened along," said the young inventor, sticking out his hand. "I'm Tom Swift Jr."

The lieutenant's eyes widened in recognition at the name. "That explains a lot!" He grinned.

After landing the Navy pilot at the reserve base,

where his cycloplane caused a sensation, Tom returned to Swift Enterprises. To his delight, Ed Longstreet had just arrived and was waiting for him at the hangar, accompanied by Tom's father.

"Ed's going with you," said Mr. Swift. "Well, son, is this plane up to expectations?"

"Even better, Dad!"

"Well, we leave tomorrow," Tom said to his cousin.

As they drove to the Swifts' office, Ed asked whether the cycloplane would be named.

"Yes," Tom replied. "I'm calling it the *Drumhawk*."

"Good name," his father said. As they climbed out of the jeep a few minutes later, he added, "And now, Tom, get ready for a surprise. Follow me!"

CHAPTER XV

A SLIPPERY SMUGGLER

MYSTIFIED, Tom and Ed followed the elder scientist into the Swifts' private office.

Here Mr. Swift flicked an electronic dial and beamed open a safe. Reaching inside, he took out a small, shimmering yellow-orange statue.

"Why, it's the animal god! The stolen figure!" Tom exclaimed, seizing it eagerly.

"Where did you get it?" Ed cried.

Mr. Swift explained that the police had recovered it. They had traced the masked man who had hired Jake the Cat to commit the theft.

"They still don't know his real identity," Tom's father went on, "but he was using the alias of John Aider. There's no doubt that he's our man. He speaks with a foreign accent, and pronounces the name John as *Zhohn*."

"You mean the authorities don't actually have him in custody?" Ed asked.

"Unfortunately, no. He was traced to a rooming house in Seattle. But when the police knocked on his door to arrest him, he got away via the fire escape. In his haste, however, he had to leave the statue behind."

"Say, that reminds me!" Tom burst out. Groping in the pocket of his slacks, he produced several of the stone missiles.

Mr. Swift examined the yellow-orange pellets with intense interest. "Why, they're holmium, the same as the statue, aren't they?"

"I think so, Dad. I'll put one of the stones in a spectroscope to make sure."

As the three hurried to the nearest laboratory, Ed asked, "Where did they come from?"

"A jungle attack," Tom explained. "They're probably the rarest missiles on earth."

Several of them were analyzed under the spectrograph and proved to be made of holmium.

Ed was impressed by this latest discovery. "Then your guess was right, Tom! The statue did come from New Guinea!"

"Not only that, but apparently somewhere close to the spot where Bud and Hank crashed." With a grim look, Tom added, "If there *is* a rare earths deposit there, it's being well guarded. And certain people are mighty eager to keep us from finding it!"

"Would the natives know the value of that sort of thing?" Ed inquired dubiously.

"No, but a white man might." In support of this theory, Tom reported the mysterious broadcast which he and Chow had picked up over the walkie-talkie.

Mr. Swift was worried. "That man whose voice you heard may be tied up in some way with John Aider. If so, he probably won't stop at anything. Tom, you and your rescue team must protect yourselves in every possible way!"

"We'll be on guard every minute," Tom promised. "By the way, have the police found out how the statue got into this country?"

"The customs men think that it was smuggled in, in an air freight shipment from Hollandia on the north coast of New Guinea. The airline and the flight crew involved are all in the clear, however."

Tom hoped for further developments in the case by morning, but none came. Eager to be off on his rescue mission, he took personal charge of all last-minute details. The *Kangaroo Kub* and the *Skeeter* had already been removed from the *Sky Queen's* hangar compartment, and now the cycloplane was loaded aboard.

By eleven o'clock the Flying Lab was ready to take the air. It was then that Tom noticed Bill Bennings and Herb Shawk were not there. He sent out a call over the public-address system.

In response, a mechanic in coveralls came running up. "Skipper, Bennings and Shawk hopped down to Baltimore. Didn't you know?"

"*What!*" Tom was stunned.

"Sure. Said you sent a message to take a week's rest."

Mr. Swift and Ed Longstreet looked at Tom in

amazement. The young inventor had clenched his fists in anger.

"That message was a fake!" he declared. "Our enemies, whoever they are, have pulled another fast one!"

"You'll just have to find a substitute crew," Mr. Swift commented in a troubled voice.

Over the loud-speaker, employees with flight experience were asked to report at the Flying Lab. In a few minutes fifty men had assembled.

Quickly Tom explained his predicament to them. "Who'll volunteer to come with me?"

The men shuffled their feet and looked around awkwardly, but no one stepped forward.

Both Tom and Mr. Swift were shocked. The elder scientist spoke to the group. "Are none of you willing to accompany Tom on a mission as important as this?"

Again there was silence. Then a weather-beaten, sandy-haired mechanic spoke up. "From what we hear, that New Guinea jungle's a deathtrap."

Tom's eyes flashed angrily. "I look fairly healthy, don't I? And Bennings and Shawk came back in good shape, too. Sure, a jungle rescue mission is no picnic, but it needn't be too dangerous if we use our common sense. The point is, Bud Barclay and Hank Sterling are depending on us to save their lives. When a friend's in that kind of trouble, you don't count the cost. Now who'll come with me?"

Tom's words seemed to strike home. Many of

the men flushed and visibly straightened up. This time, over a dozen volunteers stepped forward.

The young inventor gave them a quiet smile. "Thanks for the vote of confidence, fellows. I'd like to take all of you—but Enterprises can spare only two men right now to accompany me."

After selecting two mechanics in their early twenties, Tom gave them fifteen minutes to get ready and dismissed the others.

At last the crewmen climbed aboard and Tom took his place at the controls. He gunned the Flying Lab at top speed and again managed to outrun the sun. It was still morning when the huge plane reached the vicinity of the twin extinct volcanoes.

Turning on the radio, Tom beamed out a signal. Almost immediately he made contact with Slim's group.

"We saw you coming, skipper!" Slim exclaimed. In the background Tom could hear the joyful comments of the other members of the rescue party. "We're plenty glad you're back."

"How goes it down there?" Tom asked.

"Well, we're still on our feet," Slim reported wryly. "Two more attacks from the stone throwers since you left."

"Any casualties?"

"No, just a few sore shins and heads. We've lost some grub, though, to jungle cockroaches. They're worse than any savages!"

Tom asked how close the men were to the spot where their pals had crashed.

"We figure about six miles," Slim replied.

"How's the terrain? Still pretty bad?"

"Terrible!" Slim groaned. "If it gets any worse, we may need blasting powder to get through! But we intend to keep pushing ahead," he added.

"Swell, Slim," Tom said. "Good luck, now! And keep in touch!"

"Roger!"

After signing off, Tom swooped down over the treetops to his previous landing spot. Hardly had the *Sky Queen* touched ground, when Chow and Arv came bursting out of the bushes to greet them.

"Brand my goggles, you're a sight fer sore eyes, boy!" the cook exclaimed.

"Longest two days we've ever spent," Hanson added.

Tom introduced his cousin Ed to the men, explained why Bennings and Shawk had not returned, and told about the statue having been located.

Chow grunted. "So them varmints are closin' in on us, eh?"

Arv set his jaw. "With Tom back, I'd say we're closing in on them!" He now reported how the two natives had picked up the walkie-talkie and then disappeared into the jungle, leaving no trace.

"We tried to warn Slim," Hanson went on, "but we couldn't make contact."

"They're okay," said Tom.

After getting the others to help him roll the

cycloplane out of the *Sky Queen's* hangar compartment, Tom took off alone on his first reconnaissance flight.

The storm was still raging around the volcanoes. Remembering his recent test flight, however, Tom approached the area confidently.

The sleek little craft responded perfectly as he came down through the overcast. Again and again, bursts of rain lashed his canopy, while gale winds howled on all sides. But this time Tom was piloting a ship which defied the elements!

Slowly and smoothly he descended between the twin volcanoes. He was lower now than ever before. Peering through the semidarkness, he made out a cluster of huts.

"A native village," he noted in silent surprise. "And look at those roofs! They're every color of the rainbow!"

Suddenly Tom interrupted his mental observations as he realized the *Drumhawk* was becoming sluggish. A glance at the flight dials sent a chill of fear through him. The needles were flickering crazily. The instruments had gone haywire!

CHAPTER XVI

A GRIM DISCOVERY

FRANTICALLY Tom increased the output of the ultrasonic generator that powered the sonic turbines. Finally the rotating cylinders responded by increasing speed.

Bit by bit, the cycloplane rose higher, as if straining against an invisible cable. At last it soared free above the overcast. With a gasp of relief Tom gunned the jet engines and the plane shot forward out of danger.

"Whew!" Tom's heart pounded. "Another minute and I'd have crashed just as Bud and Hank did!"

At top speed he took the cycloplane back to the jungle clearing.

"What happened?" Arv asked, worried.

"I've just found out why Bud and Hank crashed!" the young inventor told him. "The plane was okay through the storm area, then suddenly the instruments and control system were fouled up. I think it was caused by a high-powered electromagnetic field, probably triggered by radar whenever a plane approaches the valley."

"Good night!" gasped Arv. "Then someone has set up a deliberate trap!"

"Right," Tom agreed. "Someone with a highly scientific mind."

Chow smacked his gnarled fist against his open palm. "I'll bet it's the same hombre we heard over my walkie-talkie!"

Tom nodded. "I'm sure of it, Chow. Remember what he said? *'The charge is working to perfection. We're ready for the capture.'* "

The men stared at one another in consternation as the full impact of the news sank in. Tom, meanwhile, was striding back and forth, his hands plunged deep in the pockets of his jeans.

"What's the answer, Tom?" asked Ed Longstreet. "Does that mean we're licked?"

"Far from it." Tom halted, his blue eyes flashing. "We can protect the cycloplane against any more attacks and then make another trip. We'll coat it with Tomasite. I'm sure it will shield the plane from this type of electrical radiation."

"Yahoo!" Chow let out a Comanche war whoop, followed by a jubilant chuckle. "By jingo, I knew them sidewinders couldn't stop us fer long!"

"Don't celebrate too soon, Chow," Tom cautioned. "I still have to find a way to protect us after we land. Let me give it some thought. In the meantime, how about you fellows mixing some Tomasite and spraying it on the cycloplane?"

"Roger!"

The young inventor hurried aboard the Flying Lab to work on the new problem. In the electronics cubicle he covered sheet after sheet of paper with hasty computations and sketches of transistorized circuits.

"No go," he told himself over and over again.

His working space, lighted by the soft glow of a fluorescent lamp, was one of several partitioned units in the laboratory compartment of the huge ship. He got up and strolled through the chemical unit, the biology and botany cubicles, deep in thought.

It was an hour later when the young inventor burst out of the *Sky Queen's* hatch into the jungle clearing.

"I have it, Ed! I have it!"

With eager smiles the others swarmed up to listen.

"Well, it all goes back to Maxwell's equations," Tom began. "If we assume the wave length of the electromagnetic radiation produced by the—"

"Who-o-oa! Hold it, pardner!" Chow protested. "I kin bust a bronc, but I sure can't stick in the saddle when you start spoutin' them jawbreakers!"

"Okay, Chow." Tom laughed. "What it all boils down to is this: I've doped out a small gadget—you might call it a *resistorizer,* I guess— powered by one of my flashlight-size solar-charged batteries."

"What's it do?" asked one of the men.

"Very roughly, it automatically throws out a

counterwave of its own," Tom explained. "This wave is always 180 degrees out of phase with any electromagnetic wave and will dissipate the energy of our enemy's weapon in a burst of tremendous heat."

The announcement brought a surge of cheers.

"Will one of these gadgets do the trick for all of us?" Ed asked.

"No," Tom replied. "Each of us had better carry one, to be on the safe side. I can rig up a dozen pretty fast."

Returning to the laboratory, Tom laid out tiny transistors, wire, batteries, pieces of lead, and began assembling them at top speed with his midget pocket-pencil soldering iron. As housings for the resistorizers, he used small plastic containers from the chemical lab. These, in turn, received a coat of Tomasite.

By night the job was done. Hurrying out to the clearing once again, Tom handed one of the protective devices to each man, then stuffed the rest into his jungle kit.

"Cycloplane's sprayed," Arv reported. "It will be ready for take-off in the morning."

Early the following day Tom announced, "Sorry, but I can't take more than two men with me. Otherwise I won't have room to bring back Hank and Bud. Besides, there should be a crew here to guard the *Sky Queen*."

Ed Longstreet would be needed on the rescue team in case they had to talk with the natives. For his other crewmate Tom picked Chow. Arv agreed that he could help best by standing ready to pilot the Flying Lab in case of emergency. The two flight crewmen would help him man the huge ship and operate the radio equipment.

Tom, Ed, and Chow climbed aboard the *Drumhawk* and once again Tom headed for the extinct volcanoes. The ever-present turbulence hit the cycloplane, but the ship descended through it with hardly a tremor.

"What about the electrical field?" Ed Longstreet asked in a tense voice, as the floor of the valley came into view. "Will we know when it comes on?"

Tom shook his head. "Not necessarily. It was about here that the plane went out of control before. I imagine we've already triggered our enemy's device, but the Tomasite coating's protecting us."

His eyes scanned the village below. There was not a sign of life. Again the huts' thatched roofs, gleaming iridescently in rainbow hues, held his interest. Could it be that—

He was interrupted by Chow. "Look, you fellers! There it is!"

He pointed to the starboard slope of one volcano. At the very foot of the cliff, half-hidden among the rocks and underbrush, lay a crumpled silver mass. It was the wreckage of Bud and Hank's cargo jet!

In grim silence, the rescue trio eyed the smashed plane as their own craft settled downward to the valley floor. One wing of the cargo plane had been almost completely sheared by the impact.

No one dared voice the thought that shot through all three minds. *Had the jet carried Bud and Hank to their doom after all?*

The instant the cycloplane's wheels touched ground, Tom killed the switch. As the tense searchers started to jump out, he said:

"Hold on! No use in all of us taking a chance with that electrical radiation. I'll go and see if the resistorizer works against it."

Hopping out, Tom hurried toward the wreckage. He felt no shock. Either the strange electrical equipment was not turned on or his gadget was a perfect repeller. The young inventor waved the others to follow him.

Anxiously they poked among the wreckage, but found no trace of any bodies. Tom straightened up with a thoughtful frown. Apparently their two missing friends had been carried off, either dead or alive. But where? And what had happened to the native villagers?

"It's like a ghost town," said Ed.

Tom nodded. The whole valley lay wrapped in a foreboding stillness.

CHAPTER XVII

THE SECRET NOTE

TOM and his companions were more conscious of the air of mystery that hung over the valley than they cared to admit.

"Let's investigate the village," said Tom finally.

Warily he led the way, with Ed and Chow following. Their eyes scanned the rocks and underbrush.

"I reckon them natives might try to bushwhack us," said Chow.

"Not only that, but the scientist who sends out that electric radiation may try something else even worse," Tom replied.

Nothing broke the stillness as they approached the nearest huts. The walls of the dwellings were made of stakes planted in a circle and joined by woven strands of reeds.

The trio peered cautiously into several huts, but found each one dark and empty. Tumbled gourds, eating implements, straw mats, and scattered items of food, such as bananas and yams, seemed to indicate a hasty exit.

In one hut Tom found a gorgeous native headdress made of orange and green bird-of-paradise feathers. Why had the owner left such a treasure?

"Looks as if he and the others cleared out fast," Ed Longstreet remarked.

Tom nodded. "The question is why? Because we broke through their electrical defense system?"

Everything indicated a crude, primitive mode of life, not in keeping with that of a scientist. The hut floors were of trampled earth, while the streets of the village themselves were mere beaten tracks among the rows of dwellings. At the very center of the group of huts was an open stone fireplace, surrounded by a circle of boulders.

"Probably where they hold their village feasts and ceremonial dances," Ed commented, then asked, "What's our next move, Tom?"

"We'll try to get in touch with Slim and the land party," Tom decided. "Let's get the transmitter that's tuned to the set Slim has and set it up in one of these huts. We don't dare use the walkie-talkie wave band."

Returning to the cycloplane, Chow brought the radio to the nearest hut. Tom turned it on.

"You two stay in the hut and keep beaming out a signal till you raise Slim," he told his companions. "I'll scout around and see if I can dig up any clues to what's going on here."

After half an hour of fruitless probing, Tom paused. Once again his eyes fell on the thatched roofs, with their amazing mixture of colors. The hues ranged through the whole spectrum—from a shimmering violet, blue, and blue-green to yellow-orange and a queer metallic red.

Standing on tiptoe, Tom plucked a handful of thatching from the nearest hut. A closer look left him wide-eyed with amazement. The stuff was even more fantastic than he had imagined! He rolled some of it between his fingers.

"Mineral fibers!" he muttered. But the stuff was far different from asbestos or any similar material known to modern science.

There was only one answer. It must be a combination of rare earths! "Probably in the form of silicates," Tom reflected with growing excitement. "Is that why Bud and Hank sent that radio message with the word 'rare'?" he asked himself.

Brushing aside the gloomy fear that his friends might not be alive, the young inventor's thoughts went racing eagerly into the future. What research could be carried out with a new and plentiful supply of rare earths! Experiments leading to revolutionary advances in the field of atomic energy, new electronic devices; stronger and more heat-resistant metal alloys!

"It doesn't add up though," Tom reflected, looking at the huts. "How could primitive stone-age natives separate those rare earths?"

With a shrug, Tom dismissed the knotty problem from his mind. Right now the main thing was to find a clue to Bud and Hank's fate. The young inventor resumed his search of the huts. It was several minutes later when a gleam of reflected light inside one of the dwellings caught his eye.

Tom pounced on the object which lay on a woven green and yellow mat. It was Bud Barclay's wrist watch! Hardly two feet away was Hank Sterling's!

Tom's heart gave a leap. Both watches were still running, their crystals unshattered. If the watches had survived the crash in good shape, more than likely his friends had, too! It looked almost certain now that Bud and Hank had spent some time in the village. Both were probably alive!

Then another thought occurred to Tom. If, by any chance, his friends had left their watches here in the hope that they might be noticed by a rescue party, perhaps they had taken other steps, too. Maybe Bud and Hank had tried to leave some kind of message in the gloomy hut!

Tom whipped out his flashlight and played it around the room. At first glance nothing of interest showed up. Undaunted, he began a thorough search, poking into every nook and cranny.

At one spot the dirt floor had been dug up, then hastily covered over. But the corner of a sheet of white paper was still visible.

Tom clawed away the dirt and pulled out the paper. A note from Bud! With pounding pulse, the young scientist read:

Tom:
Hank and I are alive and okay so far (the 17th), but we're prisoners of a white man who seems to have the natives under his power. Tomorrow morning they are taking us to a cave to keep you

His pulse pounding, Tom read the message

from finding us. They tell us we'll never be allowed to leave. And if you find out what the white man is doing, you'll be put to death! So long and here's hoping you find this.

Bud

As he read the news, Tom was both relieved and angry. Not only would he find Bud and Hank, but he would unlock the valley's secret!

"Today's only the 18th," he thought jubilantly.

Stuffing the paper into his pocket, Tom hurried back to the hut where he had left Ed and Chow. A voice was coming from the radio.

"It's Slim!" Ed cried out. "He and the others are less than a mile from here!"

Grabbing up the mike, Tom exclaimed, "That's wonderful, Slim! In fact it's terrific!"

"But we're worried, Tom."

"What about?"

"Hedron's missing!" Slim answered.

"How come?"

"Well, he offered to do some scouting for us, while we stopped to eat. So I said okay. But that was over half an hour ago and he still hasn't come back. I'm plenty worried, skipper!"

Tom frowned. "Have you tried to find him or called on the walkie-talkie?"

"Both. No response. We can't even—"

Suddenly the crew chief's voice broke off with a gasp. In the background an outburst of shouts and frightened yells could be heard.

"Slim!" Tom cried. "What's happening?"

"We're being attacked!"

CHAPTER XVIII

BATTLE REPORT

THERE WAS no further word from Slim; just faint, confused yelling. Then that, too, died away amid the crackle of radio static. Anxiously Tom and Ed hovered over the set, hoping for more information about the attack.

Chow, however, was roused to fighting fury by the news. "Brand my sunfishin' bronc," he sputtered angrily, "I'll show them jungle rustlers!"

Before his two companions could stop him, the tough old Texan went charging out the door, yelling a wild Indian war whoop. It took Tom a second to recover from his surprise. Then he leaped into action.

"Chow! Come back!" he called out. "You couldn't get there in time to do any good!"

The cook glanced back over his shoulder, his weathered face red with rage and excitement, but continued running. "Goin' to wipe out them varmints, that's what!" he hollered. "I'll show 'em how a Texas cowboy handles a bunch o' skulkin', back-shootin' coyotes! *Ya-hoo!*"

Hauling out his machete and waving it like a cutlass, he galloped forward.

"Chow!" Tom started after him, then gave up as the cook reached the edge of the forest.

Ed Longstreet, who had followed Tom, laid a hand on his shoulder. "Let Chow go. His fighting blood's up! Besides," he added thoughtfully, "it might just do some good. So stop worrying about him."

Tom, feeling that he himself could not arrive at the battle scene in time to be of service, reluctantly turned back. "I believe we might give some assistance by getting a fuller radio report," he said.

Back at the hut, they began signaling urgently to Slim, but he did not reply. Either he had switched off his radio and fled, or else his transmitter had been knocked out of commission.

With a sigh Tom said, "Even if that's hopeless, there's one thing I can do." Pulling out the two watches and Bud's note, he related how he had found them in one of the huts. "I'm going to look for that cave Bud mentioned. You keep working the radio."

As Ed glanced at the towering volcanic peaks on either side of the valley, he said, "Bud and Hank are alive! Thank goodness! And they're somewhere inside those mountains!"

"I have a hunch the cave is fairly close to the village," Tom mused. "I'll try the eastern side first."

"Good luck!" said his cousin.

Tom trudged toward the rocky lava-hardened slope. When he reached a point where the ground ahead rose steeply, he began skirting along the edge. The going was rough, but he soon progressed far beyond sight of the village. However, he found no trace of a cave entrance.

"Must be in the other volcano," Tom told himself.

He headed back toward the cluster of huts to see if there was news of the battle. As he passed through the village, he noticed that one dwelling was considerably larger than the others.

"Must be the chief's hut," he decided.

Poking his head in the doorway, he switched on his flashlight and played it around the interior. He caught his breath in surprise. In a corner stood a small, curious-looking statue.

Tom rushed in and grabbed it. Except for its metallic violet color, the figurine was a duplicate of the "animal god" now locked in his father's office safe!

"It's true!" Tom thought jubilantly. "That statue in Shopton did come from this part of New Guinea. It probably was stolen out of this very hut!"

But stolen by whom? Tom wondered. John Aider? Or the mysterious white man who was now holding Bud and Hank prisoner?

"Maybe the two of them are working together!" the young inventor speculated.

Eager to report his latest discovery, Tom headed back on the double to the radio hut. Ed

Longstreet listened in amazement to his cousin's report, then gave some news of his own.

"The battle's over, Tom! I got Slim again."

"What happened?"

"I'm not sure. It was pretty violent, I guess, but apparently everyone survived. Slim's checking up right now."

In a few moments the crew chief returned to the air. "All safe and accounted for!" he reported.

Tom grabbed up the mike. "Anyone hurt?"

"Not too bad," Slim replied. "Doc's patching up the cuts and bruises. Three of our walkie-talkies got smashed. Those stones sure were whizzing in. Luckily the transmitter's still working. I lugged it behind a big boulder after I signed off."

"Good work, Slim!" Tom congratulated him. "Did Chow get there?"

"No. Haven't seen him."

"He's on his way. Look for him."

"Okay. And another thing, skipper. Hedron's on his way back. Picked up a call from him just a minute ago. Says he almost walked into the middle of the stone barrage, but saw what was going on and ducked for cover till the attack was over."

Tom frowned. "Slim, did it ever occur to you that Hedron's either awfully lucky or awfully smart?"

"What do you mean, skipper?"

"Every time there's been an attack, he's managed to disappear just before it happened."

There was silence for a moment, then Slim

said excitedly, "That's right! Tom, you mean he might be in cahoots with these natives?"

"There's someone else besides natives mixed up in this," Tom replied. Quickly he told Slim about the mysterious white man whose voice he and Chow had overheard—and also about Bud's earlier distrust of George Hedron.

"Let's not take any chances," the young inventor concluded, his suspicion growing. "When Hedron shows up, take his walkie-talkie away from him! And keep your big set turned on every minute!"

"Roger!"

Tom turned back to his cousin. "Take over, Ed. I'm going to hunt for that cave again."

This time, Tom headed toward the western edge of the valley. Again he skirted the cliff wall. The terrain was strewn with rocks and brush.

For fifteen minutes Tom tramped along without finding anything. Suddenly he was startled by a small creature which popped up almost in front of his face. He recognized it as a kangaroo rat. To his astonishment, it disappeared right before his eyes!

"What goes on here?" the young inventor muttered, stopping abruptly.

With a surge of excitement, he clawed among the brush, eager to uncover the tiny kangaroo's secret. A whole cluster of shrubbery came away in his hand. Beyond yawned an opening.

"The cave!" Tom gasped.

Plunging into the dark interior, he snapped on his flashlight. The glow revealed several large rawhide sacks set just inside the entrance.

Tom opened one eagerly and whistled softly in amazement. The sack was full of weird treasures! Idols, statuettes, vases, and an assortment of strange objects glistened in metallic rainbow colors!

"More rare earths!" Tom exclaimed.

He aimed his flashlight deeper into the gloom. No rear wall was apparent. Instead, a path sloped downward into yawning darkness.

"This must be the entrance to an underground storehouse of treasures!" Tom gasped.

CHAPTER XIX

AN AMAZING CAVERN

FOR A MOMENT Tom was tempted to plunge forward and find out where the underground path led. But caution held him back. He might be walking into a deadly trap!

"This will take careful planning," he decided. Pulsing with excitement, Tom hurried back to the hut where Ed was manning the radio.

His cousin burst out, "I just heard from Slim! They've met Chow, and he's leading them here. They should arrive in half an hour."

Tom gave a joyful whoop. "Now we can really get moving!" As a thought came to him, he added, "Is Hedron with them?"

Longstreet shook his head. "He didn't show up and they haven't heard from him. Funny thing is, he was supposed to be traveling in the same direction the others were. But so far they haven't found a trace of him."

Tom frowned as he dropped his kit bag onto the floor and squatted down beside the radio. "Looks as if Bud had Hedron's number, all right."

"Sure does," Ed agreed. "Slim's afraid Hedron might even be arranging with the natives for an ambush!"

"Boy, let's hope not!" Tom muttered. "Now let me tell you some *good* news!"

"You found the cave?" Ed asked.

"Right." Quickly Tom related what he had discovered in the slope of the volcano, including the rawhide bags of rare earths objects.

Longstreet received the news with mixed emotions. He congratulated Tom on the find, then said, "This sounds like a dangerous setup. Suppose our enemy's at the other end of the tunnel!"

Tom's blue eyes blazed with determination. "Suppose he is. We still have to rescue Bud and Hank. Don't worry," he went on. "We'll watch our step and wear our resistorizers. That ought to make it safe."

Ed relaxed and smiled. "I guess I can count on that twenty-four-carat brain of yours to figure out all the facets."

Tom grinned. "Okay, I'll concentrate on our enemy's game. Let's hope they don't pitch us a curve!"

Tom reached over to the radio and tuned it to the *Sky Queen's* frequency. "Might as well brief Arv while we're waiting. Rescue flight calling *Sky Queen!* . . . Can you read me, Arv?"

Hanson's voice came back almost immediately. "Sure can, Tom. What's new?"

When Tom told him, Hanson whistled. "For Pete's sake, take it easy in that cave. By the way, your father called. He said to tell you the police have finally arrested that guy John Aider."

"Great!" said Tom. "Has he done any talking yet?"

"Plenty. But the cops think most of it's a lot of malarkey. Aider says that the statue belongs to him and he wants it back. He claims that he lost it in San Francisco and tracked it all the way to the Shopton Museum.

"And he also says—get this"—Arv's voice became sarcastic—"Aider says he's very sorry he hired a burglar to steal it back. But the statue belongs to him, so what's the difference?"

Tom smiled grimly at the crook's brazen attitude. "Might make a difference of several years in prison I should think!"

Just then a faint sound of shouts and excited voices came drifting in through the doorway. Ed rushed out to look.

"It's Chow and the land party!" he called back.

Tom reported this to Arv and added, "I'd better sign off now!"

Tom hurried outside and was surrounded by a howling, back-slapping, bear-hugging quartet of dirty, sunburned jungle hikers.

"All right, all right, give Tom air, you wranglers!" Chow bawled at them.

As the men relaxed their embraces, Tom shook hands warmly with each one. "Man alive, you're really a sight for sore eyes!" he exclaimed.

"We're a sight, all right!" joked Sam Barker. With their trail-worn khaki, unshaven faces, and arms covered with cuts and insect bites, legs wrapped in mud-caked bandages, the men looked as though they had been months instead of days away from civilization.

"Just call us the four jungle bums!" Doc Simpson chuckled.

"Anyhow, we're sure glad to see you, skipper!" Slim declared, slapping Tom's shoulder.

"You can say that again!" Red Jones chimed in. "And plenty doggone glad to be out of that bush!"

"Too bad I can't offer you any armchairs or iced drinks," Tom said, then introduced Ed Longstreet. "I'm sorry to tell you, but the toughest job probably still lies ahead, fellows."

Quickly he briefed them on the various discoveries he had made since the cycloplane landed. Overjoyed to hear Bud and Hank were alive, the men bristled with anger when Tom told them that the two were being held prisoner.

"What are we waiting for!" Slim exploded. "Let's go after them right now!"

As they cleaned up a bit and ate, Tom mapped out a plan of action. Slim and Red were detailed to guard the cycloplane, to make sure sneak raiders did not destroy it while the rescuers of Bud and Hank were gone. Sam was assigned to act as watchdog in the headquarters hut. In case the stone throwers tried to infiltrate the village in a surprise attack, he could notify the *Drumhawk*. The cycloplane, in turn, could go to the Flying Lab for reinforcements. The rest of the group would handle the rescue operations in the cave. "But first," Tom said, "I want each of you newcomers to take one of these."

Reaching into his kit, he pulled out the extra resistorizers he had made and explained how the device worked. Then he handed one apiece to Slim, Doc, Sam, and Red.

"Keep it turned on at all times," he warned. "Our unseen enemy might spray us with another electrical barrage when we're least expecting it!"

Before embarking on their rescue mission, Tom and his group made a trip to the cycloplane for special equipment in case of emergency. They picked up gas masks for every man plus two extra for Bud and Hank, fire-extinguisher capsules, several coils of light nylon rope, and infrared snooperscopes and viewers for each searcher. These snooperscopes, which were pocket size and looked like blue pencils, were capable of sending out an infrared light strong enough to reveal, when seen through the viewer, the outline of any object in inky dark surroundings.

"All set!" Tom called.

He had marked the location of the cave entrance with stones, so his party found the spot without difficulty. Pulling aside the shrubbery, they groped their way into the gloomy interior.

"Here's the treasure I was telling you about," Tom said, playing his flashlight over the rawhide sacks.

The men gasped as they opened one and examined its iridescent contents.

"I wonder why the natives stored it here?" Doc Simpson asked, admiring a weird-shaped bird of bluish-green metal.

"I have a hunch that it was a white man who gathered these objects," Tom replied. "And not because he likes primitive art, either. Don't forget this stuff is made out of rare earths—and is worth a fortune for research purposes. He's probably figuring on shipping the objects back to civilization."

To frustrate their enemy's scheme, Tom's

The trio gasped in amazement when they

group hauled the bags outside the cave and hid them deep in the underbrush.

"You'd better stay here and guard this cave entrance, Chow," said Tom, "in case of an attack from the rear."

"You sure you don't want old Chow to come along with you down that there tunnel?" asked the Texan, unhappy at being parted from his young boss.

"You're needed right here, Chow," Tom assured him earnestly. "I'm counting on you to

sighted the ancient underground city

make sure that no one sneaks up and gets the drop on us while our backs are turned. It could prove to be a dangerous assignment, if they try anything."

The grizzled cowpoke brightened. "Reckon you kin count on me to keep any sneakin' varmints out o' here," he promised.

The others started through the mysterious tunnel. To guide them, they beamed the infrared rays of the snooperscopes, which revealed the pathway ahead in ghostly outlines.

For some time they picked their way along in silence through the narrow, winding passageway. Every step took them deeper underground. The eerie darkness and the rocky walls closing them in tightly on either side began to get on Ed's nerves.

"Doesn't this thing *ever* end?" he whispered.

Suddenly they detected a glow of light, somewhere ahead.

"Oh, oh! We're coming to something!" muttered Doc Simpson tensely.

A few minutes later they gasped in amazement as the tunnel widened into an enormous cavern as bright as daylight. Before them lay an ancient underground city!

CHAPTER XX

CRIES FOR HELP

ED LONGSTREET was the first to find his voice.
"Great Scott! This is fantastic!" he murmured.
"If I weren't seeing it with my own eyes, I
wouldn't believe it!"

All three stared in awe at the incredible scene
spread out before them. Sometime in the long
distant past, an unknown race of stone masons
had built this whole city deep down under the
earth.

"But why?" Tom asked himself. "And what
lights it up?"

There were houses shaped like pyramids,
domed temples, public buildings with high arched
doorways, and walls covered with strange carvings.
Here and there, mounted on pedestals, were
brooding statues like that of the animal god back
in Shopton.

Strangest of all were the streets, with deep-
carved grooves as if made to be used as tracks
for wheeled carts or chariots.

Once, the visitors realized, the city had

141

throbbed with life—busy, bustling throngs of people. Now the buildings were deserted, the streets covered with a thick, gritty layer of dust and debris.

"But where's the light coming from?" Doc puzzled aloud.

The strange glow that made every object visible bathed the whole city in a weird, unearthly radiance. Every building stood out in soft silhouette.

Tom admitted he was baffled. "The light is coming from somewhere beyond the city, perhaps from the far end of the cavern!"

His own interest was focused on the stone of which the houses and other buildings were constructed. Rainbow colors, in a sort of speckled pattern, shone iridescently throughout the surface of the stone.

Tom flicked on his flashlight and examined the stones at close range. "These colored veins look like more of the rare earths!" he muttered.

Ed was staggered by the announcement. "Do you mean the whole city's *built* out of the stuff?"

"Out of the ore," Tom corrected. "There must be a huge quarry somewhere around here!"

In awe-struck silence the trio pushed forward through the deserted streets. Still there was no sign of life. Only their own echoing footsteps broke the stillness of the great cavern.

Suddenly Tom gasped and halted. "Hold it!" he told the others, and aimed his flashlight downward.

The yellow glow revealed bare footprints in the dusty litter of the street!

Doc gasped. "Do you suppose these are the undisturbed footprints of people who lived here centuries ago?"

Tom pondered this. "No. But they may be prints of the savages who—"

"Help! Help!"

The faint cries had come from somewhere ahead of them.

"Come on!" Tom cried. "Maybe that's Bud or Hank!"

The trio dashed forward, picking their way through the maze of winding streets. As they ran, all of them kept alert for an ambush. Apparently the place was not deserted after all! There might be an onslaught of savages or a rain of stone missiles at any moment.

But nothing happened.

Finally they slowed to a walk, then halted. Without the cries to guide them, it was impossible for the rescuers to tell if they were heading in the right direction.

Ed looked at Tom. "Do you think that call was a trap?"

"I'd rather not guess," Tom replied, "but I certainly intend to find out. Let's—"

His words were interrupted as a voice behind them suddenly called out, "Hi, you fellows!"

The three rescuers whirled around as if they had been stung. To their amazement, George Hedron was strolling toward them!

His manner was completely casual. Ignoring their wide-eyed looks of surprise, he greeted them with a smile. The man acted as if there were nothing unusual about meeting them here in this underground city.

"Do you mind telling us where you've been all this time?" Tom asked sharply.

"Of course not. Guess I owe you an apology about that," Hedron replied. "The fact is, I pulled another one of my harebrained stunts. Saw a baby kangaroo while I was out scouting and thought maybe I could bag it. Never did, though —it finally got away. By that time I realized I was lost. But luckily," he concluded, "I managed to find the trail again, and here I am."

As the others eyed him coldly without speaking, Hedron merely grinned. "Don't worry," he added, "I've really learned my lesson! Next time I'll follow orders."

"And how did you happen to find us down here?" Tom asked.

"Oh, Slim and Chow told me where you were," Hedron replied smoothly. Looking around at the ancient buildings, he went on, "Isn't this an amazing spot? I've never seen or heard of anything like it!"

Before Tom could comment, the plea for help was suddenly repeated.

"Must be your friends!" Hedron exclaimed. "Come on. Let's go!"

Breaking into a run, the four men raced in the direction from which the cries had come. In a few moments they reached a spot where the narrow, twisting streets widened into a plaza or public square. With gasps of amazement, Tom and his friends pulled up short.

A fantastic scene, illumined by huge floodlights, met their eyes. Across the plaza trudged a group of dark-skinned natives in single file. Their ankles were manacled and linked by chains, while on their shoulders they bore heavily loaded sacks.

"So this is where the missing villagers have been hiding!" murmured Ed, dumfounded.

Beyond, ranged against the far wall of the cavern, stood more of the natives, oddly smeared with paint and covered with leaves. It was several seconds before Tom realized the purpose of this strange garb.

"It's for camouflage—jungle camouflage!" he told himself, then thought with a sinking heart, "Those men must be the invisible army of stone snipers!"

A STRANGE WEAPON

THIS was no time to stand in full view of the warlike natives! A deadly hail of stones might follow when their presence was discovered.

"Quick! In here!" Tom whispered to his three companions. He gestured toward the darkened doorway of one of the pyramid-shaped stone houses.

Hastily the group ducked for cover. But no sooner were they huddled inside the dwelling than Tom realized that only two of his friends had accompanied him. George Hedron was still standing outside!

"Come in here!" Tom urged him. "If those men spot us, they may attack!"

But the zoologist seemed completely unaware of any danger. Standing in plain view of the plaza, he scanned the scene with a keen, intent air.

"What's wrong with him?" Ed puzzled. "Has he gone deaf?"

Tom watched the scientist through narrowed eyes and thought, "It could be that he doesn't *want* to hear me!"

There was something odd about Hedron's attitude. He seemed poised for action—like a panther crouched to spring. By this time, Tom's distrust had grown to a near certainty that the zoologist was up to something.

Meanwhile, the present danger was too great to speculate about Hedron's motives. Any second now the jungle snipers might discover the intruders.

In a tense, heart-pounding silence, Tom and his companions waited. Nothing happened. Apparently the stone slingers still had not discovered that they were being spied upon.

"What do you make of it?" Ed asked.

"Beyond me," Doc replied.

Tom said nothing. He peered out cautiously. The column of chained natives was still plodding across the public square with their heavy loads. Either the snipers were focusing all their attention on the slaves in order to prevent any break for freedom or else they were too busy talking among themselves to notice Hedron.

Suddenly Tom gave a startled gasp. As the last few slaves trudged past, out of his line of vision, he saw two figures propped sideways against a street fountain.

"Bud! Hank!" he cried out.

Throwing caution to the winds, the young inventor rushed out of his hiding place. In the sudden surge of excitement and relief that swept over him, nothing else mattered except to reach his pals' sides!

As he raced toward the fountain, with Ed and Doc at his heels, Tom shouted words of encouragement to Bud and Hank. Both turned their heads to look, but otherwise remained motionless. What was even more strange, Bud and Hank did not give the slightest sign of recognition!

"Bud! Hank!" pleaded Tom. "Don't you know us? We're your friends!"

Neither made any response. Tom stared in horrified surprise. He saw, for the first time, that both fliers were chained. And they regarded him with a blank, unseeing gaze, as if staring into empty space!

The chained natives were still plodding across

"Steady, skipper!" Doc Simpson murmured, as Tom groaned in shocked dismay.

"Have they been brain-washed?" Ed whispered.

A thought struck Tom. "Could electric shock have done it?"

Doc nodded.

In desperation Tom glanced about the plaza, trying to figure out his best move. Another horrifying sight met his eyes. Women and children of the tribe cowered against the lofty arching walls of the cavern, apparently completely subdued.

Just then a new development caught the rescue party's attention. A small, sandy-haired white man

the public square with their heavy loads

had darted out from one of the buildings. In one hand he lugged a big, heavily laden sack.

His other arm cradled a queer-looking device like nothing Tom had ever seen before. Cylindrical in shape, it was covered with white ceramic insulation. From the front end protruded two thick electrodes which looked like the antennae of some monstrous insect.

"A weapon of some kind!" Tom concluded.

At the same moment it flashed through his mind that this man must be the mysterious scientist who kept the natives enslaved. No doubt the object under his arm was the device which he had used to shock his victims into dazed submission whenever they became rebellious.

"Quick! We must protect Bud and Hank!" Tom exclaimed to his companions.

Groping into his shoulder kit, he pulled out two resistorizers. As Doc took one for Hank, Tom himself jammed the other inside Bud's belt and flicked on the switch.

Then he remembered Hedron. He must give him one. Turning, he was just in time to see the zoologist raise one arm and shrill out the word:

"Okay!"

The next instant, Hedron started racing at top speed toward the cavern entrance.

"Hedron *is* a spy!" Tom decided.

He whirled back and saw the sandy-haired white man aiming his strange weapon straight at the rescue trio.

With an evil leer of triumph, he fired!

CHAPTER XXII

BLAZING SHOWDOWN

AN INSTANT after the unknown man pulled the trigger a bluish-white luminescent glow filled the air around the electrodes. For a few fearful seconds Tom wondered if his resistorizers would repel the attack.

Feeling no effect himself, he watched his friends. They too seemed to be all right.

Ed, relaxing a bit, said, "Tom, how does that thing work?"

"The antennae probably send out a train of electromagnetic shock waves!" Tom replied, then added swiftly, "Tell those stone throwers we come as friends—that we're not here to harm anybody! Say that if they overpower their captors, we'll set them free!"

Instantly Ed began shouting out Tom's words, first in pidgin English, then in a string of New Guinea dialects, one after the other.

But none of the translations brought the slightest response. Either the natives spoke an unknown tongue, or else they were too afraid of having the deadly ray turned on them if they responded to the pleading.

"It's hopeless!" Ed groaned, giving up at last.

Meanwhile, the bluish-white luminescent glow still filled the air around the antennae of the overseer's weapon. But fortunately it had no effect on Tom's group. Even Bud and Hank showed no evidence of further shock.

Suddenly there came a sound like a small thunderclap. A wave of heat struck them with the searing force of a furnace blast! Fearfully Tom and his companions fell back, shielding their faces against the overpowering heat.

"Wow!" choked Ed, struggling for breath. "Wh-wh-what was that?"

"Our resistorizers dissipating the shock waves!" Tom explained.

All three of the rescuers were red-faced and panting. Their lungs seemed to be on fire from the stifling effect of the hot air, but the resistorizers had protected them from being shocked into submission.

With a snarl of rage, the sandy-haired overseer seemed to realize that Tom was responsible for this. He cried out in a blistering stream of oaths, and his face twisted with fury. Then he shrieked fanatically:

"Break out the other gun!"

His cries brought two other white men hurrying from the same building. One was a stooped, skinny man with the furtive look of a half-starved wolf. The other, a huge, lumbering fellow, with muscles like a circus strong man, carried a sub-machine gun ready for action.

As he swung it up into firing position, Tom yelled a warning to his comrades, "Hit the deck!"

Not a split second too soon, they dived head-long for cover behind the fountain, pulling Bud and Hank down with them. A spray of bullets from the chattering machine gun whizzed over-head and rattled off the stone wall of a building somewhere behind them.

A choked cry came from Ed Longstreet. Tom's face went white as he glanced at his cousin. A bullet must have ricocheted and struck him!

Hoping fervently that Ed's wound was not serious, Tom fumbled in his kit. "Gas masks!" he warned. "I'm going to blast that electric field and foul up these men. Doc, you put the two extra masks on Bud and Hank!"

With his own in place, Tom produced two small fire-extinguisher capsules from his pocket. Cautiously he peered around one side of the stone fountain. The overseer was still triggering his weapon with its glowing light. Apparently he hoped that it might yet have some effect.

Taking careful aim, Tom hurled one of the capsules at the weapon. It missed by several feet.

Again he aimed and threw. This time his peg was dead on the target. As it streaked into range of the bluish-white aura, the pellet popped with a brilliant orange flash. The charge of highly com-pressed gas, released from the melted capsule, exploded into a billowing white cloud.

Instantly the sandy-haired man and his companions felt the effects of the vapor. Coughing and choking, they tried to flee. But the gas overtook them. They dropped their weapons and clutched their throats. All three stumbled and fell to their knees, then toppled face downward, unconscious.

Their collapse seemed to stun the natives. Making no sound, they stood like statues, waiting impassively.

Meanwhile, Doc Simpson had been hastily attending to Ed's injury made by the ricocheting bullet. "Only a flesh wound, so far as I can make out," he reported, and finished swabbing it with antiseptic. "How does it feel?"

"Not bad," Ed replied. "Guess the bullet just grazed my shoulder."

While Doc applied a bandage, Ed resumed his shouts to the natives. In several dialects, he told them over and over again that he and the other two rescuers had come as friends.

"You have nothing to fear!" he cried. "We wish only to help you and set you free!"

His appeals seemed to be having some effect. Although a number of the unchained natives fled, most of them stood listening in hopeful, wide-eyed awe.

As the gas cleared away, Tom rushed forward for a closer look at the three fallen white men. Doc and Ed joined him as soon as the bandaging was completed.

"Ever seen them before?" Ed asked his cousin.

Tom shook his head. "Pretty nasty customers, judging from the way they've been treating these natives—not to mention what they've done to Bud and Hank."

Stooping down, he picked up the overseer's weapon. The white ceramic insulation on the outside had cracked slightly when the device had fallen to the rocky ground from its owner's nerveless fingers.

It was still in working condition, however. When Tom aimed the cylinder in a safe direction and pressed the trigger button, it glowed as before.

"Sure is a deadly looking gadget." Ed Longstreet shuddered. "Especially when the business end was pointing our way! Could it kill a man?"

"Not likely," Tom replied. "I imagine the field is just strong enough to knock a person out at close range. What I'd like to know is how the thing's powered, but I guess that will have to wait till I have time to take it apart."

Noticing the cringing, fearful glances which the jungle snipers gave him as he fingered the weapon, Tom passed it over to Doc Simpson.

"Here, Doc, keep this trained on those stone slingers. They might just let us have it in the back again, if we don't watch them."

"I'll watch 'em! Don't worry!" Doc promised in a grim voice.

Quickly and deftly, Tom searched the fallen

white men. Their clothes contained no type of resistorizer, but in the pocket of the burly man's
dungarees Tom found a small iron key.

"Hot dog!" he exclaimed. "I'll bet it's the key
to all those manacles."

His guess proved to be correct. In a few minutes, Bud, Hank, and the native slaves had been
freed from their chains.

"Okay, let's get out of here!" Tom snapped.

"The sooner the better so far as I'm con-
cerned!" his cousin agreed fervently.

"Ditto!" put in Doc Simpson.

Issuing commands through Ed Longstreet, Tom
assigned several of the natives to carry the fallen
white men—two each for the sandy-haired overseer and the skinny, stoop-shouldered one, and
three for the hulking machine gunner. Then the
entire group of whites and natives began troop-
ing toward the cavern exit.

Tom headed the column, while Doc brought
up the rear where he could keep his shock gun
trained on the snipers. Ed Longstreet assisted
Bud and Hank, who could only stumble along
in a daze.

The march back to the outside world through
the narrow, darkened tunnel with only three
flashlights was an eerie and nerve-racking experience. Tom realized all too well that it offered a
perfect opportunity for some treacherous move
on the part of the natives. At almost any step of
the way, they might decide to rebel against their
white rescuers.

To make matters worse, there was no way of knowing what evil scheme Hedron had in mind. Even now he might be preparing some new trap or ambush for the rescue party!

As they emerged into the semigloom of the outer end of the cave, Tom gave a cry of alarm. A familiar figure lay face down just inside the entrance.

"Chow!" he exclaimed. Fearfully Tom turned him over as Ed Longstreet came hurrying to his side with a faltering question.

"Is he—is he—?"

CHAPTER XXIII

CHIEF AHTUMIK'S STORY

GRIM-FACED, Tom felt for Chow's pulse, then relaxed. "He's unconscious," the young scientist reported, "but alive. Got a terrific wallop on his head."

Gently he and Ed carried the Texan outside. The natives stared as they came from the cave and stood in a circle.

When Doc Simpson emerged at the rear of the column he handed the ray gun to Tom, then began to examine Chow.

"It must have been Hedron who hit him," said Tom. As smelling salts started to revive the cowpoke, Tom turned to Ed Longstreet. "Find Slim in the village and warn him to watch out for Hedron!"

"Righto, skipper!"

Presently Chow regained consciousness and sat up.

"How do you feel?" Tom asked with a sympathetic smile.

"Like a bull calf that jest brained hisself ag'inst a fence post!" Chow murmured.

"Did you see who hit you?"

"No. He musta snuck up behind, I reckon."

There were faint stirs and moans from the three prisoners as they gradually revived. Realizing he was tied up, the sandy-haired leader glared at his captors. About thirty years of age, he had almost colorless eyes that gave him a sinister reptilian look.

"What's the meaning of this outrage?" he hissed, as Tom held him covered with the electric shock weapon. "Do you think you can get away with this highhanded—"

"We'll ask the questions," Tom interrupted coolly. "Suppose you start by telling us your names."

"I'm Julian Strang of San Francisco, if it's any of your business," the man retorted. "These are my friends, Brad Wilkins and Len Fitch."

"Now," Tom went on, "suppose you tell us what kind of project you're engaged in here."

"We're engineers," Strang snarled. "Beyond that, we don't have to account to you for anything!"

"Engineers, eh?" Doc Simpson put in dryly. "Is that why you were making slaves of the tribe and hauling away all those ancient statues and art objects?"

"We wanted to assay their metal content, that's all," Strang said. "Any crime in that?"

"There is if you took them by force, against

the natives' consent," Tom said coldly. "What's your connection with George Hedron?"

"Never heard of him!" the overseer snapped.

"He's lyin' like a Navaho rug!" Chow growled. "That voice o' his is the same one we heard over the walkie-talkie, Tom, or my name ain't Charles Q. Winkler!"

"You're right, Chow," Tom agreed.

"Hey, here comes Ed!" Doc interrupted.

Longstreet reported that Slim Davis was safe in the headquarters hut, and that neither he nor Slim had seen Hedron.

At that moment the native chief, a stalwart black wearing a feathered headdress, broke into a volley of dialect.

"Can you understand him?" Tom asked, turning to his cousin.

Ed nodded. "He's speaking a variation of the Dani tongue. Sounds as if he doesn't like Strang, Wilkins, and Fitch. He says they're very bad men —the most evil white men he has ever known!"

"Ask him what they have been doing here," Tom requested.

Ed repeated the question in the native's dialect. There was a lengthy reply which he translated.

"Strang got lost in the jungle months ago. When the natives found him, he was out of his head with fever and almost dying. They nursed him back to health."

"Reckon that's where they made *their* big mistake!" Chow muttered sourly.

"While Strang was staying at the village," Ed went on, "he discovered the ancient underground city. Chief Ahtumik here told him that it was sacred to the tribe. Then he had a couple of natives escort Strang back to the gold mine where he works.

"But Strang must have spotted those objects made out of rare earths. Anyhow, he showed up again a few weeks later with these two goons. The natives made a big fuss over him. They thought he had come back on a friendly visit. Instead, he used the electric shock gun on them. Then he started stripping the city of everything he could carry away."

Tom's face showed the contempt he felt at Strang's treachery.

"How about these jungle snipers?" put in Doc, jerking his thumb toward the camouflaged natives. "They sure didn't act dazed, the way they sneaked up on us in the woods, trying to brain us with those stones!"

When Ed asked Ahtumik about the slingshot attacks, the chief began gesticulating angrily and speaking quickly. Ed translated.

"The white men frightened the snipers into obeying orders. Unless they attacked us and helped keep the slaves under control, their wives and children would be killed."

The chief now began to speak of his own accord.

"What's he saying?" Tom asked.

"He claims that there was someone else working for Strang—someone on the outside," Ed reported. "This person kept Strang informed of everything that was going on; told him what the land party was doing, and when a plane was getting close."

"Ask the chief if he ever saw this person," Tom probed.

"No. He says Strang got all the messages over a magic box."

"A magic box?" Tom snapped his fingers. "Strang's walkie-talkie! That's how Hedron kept in touch with him."

"Then Hedron is a double-crosser!" exclaimed Doc.

"*Hedron!* I told you that guy was no good!" a new voice spoke up.

Tom, Chow, Doc, and Ed all whirled to face the speaker. He was Bud Barclay!

"Bud! You're all right!" Tom whooped jubilantly.

His pal responded with a somewhat woozy grin, as Hank, too, showed signs that he had recovered from his state of shock. For the next few minutes, everything else was forgotten in the happy reunion of old friends. The two downed fliers were hugged, back-slapped, and hand-pumped in a frenzy of joyful relief.

"I knew you'd get through somehow, Tom," said Bud. "But in what?"

"The cycloplane." Tom gave an unrestrained grin for the first time in many days.

Bud and Hank related what had happened to

them following their crash in the turbulent, clouded valley. After being pulled out of the wreckage by Strang's men, they were held prisoner until the morning before Tom's arrival in the village. At daybreak, Strang had shocked them into a dazed stupor with his electric weapon. Neither remembered anything more until they had revived a few minutes before.

"One day while we were still in the village," said Bud, "we managed to get to our cargo plane's radio. I'd just started sending you a message, Tom, when the guards caught us and took us back to our prison hut."

Ahtumik interrupted to ask, with Ed translating, why Strang was so eager to steal the tribe's sacred idols and art objects.

Tom scratched his head. "It's going to be hard to explain to a stone-age savage, but tell him the stuff those statues are made of is valuable to the good magicians and witch doctors in our country. But we believe the bad white men were going to sell it to other people for harmful use."

This explanation seemed to satisfy the chief. He said that he would never part with the sacred objects, but the tribe would be glad to sell any of the ore that came out of the earth.

"That's wonderful," said Tom excitedly. "Now I can search for the rare earths!" Then, putting his mind on the subject at hand, he turned to Julian Strang. "Your agent back in the States has been arrested by the police. I mean the man who calls himself John Aider."

From the look of dismay that flashed into Strang's eyes, it was obvious that the news came as a bad jolt. But he merely snarled, "I don't know what you're talking about!"

"Say," Bud spoke up, "I just remembered why I was so suspicious of Hedron. When I flew home to California last Christmas, there was a picture of that guy in the San Francisco papers. He was mixed up in some shady stock deal and had to leave town."

"Too bad he got away from us here," Tom said grimly. "But he won't get far. I'll radio word to the New Guinea authorities to be on the lookout for him."

Ahtumik offered to take the "bad white men" back to his village under an all-native guard. But Tom declined the offer, afraid that the natives might take bloody vengeance on the trio.

"We'll have a couple of our men guard them," Ed translated.

In gratitude for the natives' release from slavery, Chief Ahtumik invited Tom and his friends to explore and study the underground city.

Tom smiled in anticipation. "Tell him I'll go as soon as I attend to a few things."

Before leaving the cave, Tom turned the electric shock weapon over to Chow and Hank Sterling. "Keep an eye on Strang, Wilkins, and Fitch with this until we're ready to take off."

En route back to the cycloplane, Tom stopped to ask Slim to join Chow and Hank at the cave. Reaching the plane, Bud and Hank were welcomed uproariously by Red Jones and Sam Barker.

"Sure thought that you were goners," said Red.

Tom contacted the *Sky Queen* by radio and gave Arv a full report.

"Wow!" the engineer cried. "For Pete's sake, take it easy when you go back underground!"

Before signing off, Tom asked Arv to radio a description of George Hedron to the coastal authorities. "Ask them to watch all airfields and shipping points."

"Will do, skipper!" Hanson promised.

Switching off the transmitter, Tom turned to his companions. He asked Red and Sam to guard the cycloplane in case Hedron might return.

"And now for that underground city," he said. "Bud, Doc, and Ed, want to come along?"

"Couldn't keep us away," they chorused.

After a hasty meal, the group set off. As they neared the cave, Tom remarked excitedly, "A big supply of those rare earths would be more valuable than a gold strike! And they *could* lead to revolutionary advances in scientific research!"

"Let's hope," said his cousin, "that no more trouble lies ahead."

CHAPTER XXIV

OSCILLATOR OF DOOM

WHEN they reached the cave, Tom's group stopped to speak to Chow, Slim, and Hank. Hearing the young scientist's plan, the Texan insisted the searchers take the shock gun.

"There *could* be more varmints down there, Tom," he fretted.

"What about our prisoners?" Tom asked.

"We'll hog-tie 'em with the nylon rope we ain't used yet," the cook replied.

"Okay, then," said Tom, accepting the weapon.

With Bud, Doc, and Ed following close at his heels, he headed into the tunnel. "What a place for ghosts!" Bud Barclay chuckled, as they strode through the darkness, guided by flashlights.

"How old do you suppose this lost civilization is?" Doc asked.

Ed replied, "A thousand years, maybe—at least several centuries."

Emerging into the main underground cavern, they looked through some of the pyramid-shaped houses, as well as the public buildings and temples. All were empty.

As they passed through the connecting archway, an amazing sight met their eyes. In the center of the cavern floor was a huge shallow pit, around which glowed a circle of natural light. It almost blinded them and they donned sunglasses. Nearby stood an electrical control panel, an oscillator, and an array of other modern electronic equipment!

Bud gasped. "Don't tell me the ancients had machinery like this!"

"Far from it," said Tom. "It's all brand new —installed, I'll bet, by Julian Strang!"

"But what is it?" puzzled Doc Simpson.

"The air-defense setup for guarding the valley," Tom replied. "In other words, the gear that made Bud's plane crash and almost wrecked the cycloplane!"

Most amazing of all, a stream of daylight poured down on the group from a funnel-shaped opening high overhead.

"Well, I'll be a jug-eared jet!" Bud muttered. "We must be standing at the bottom of the volcano!"

"Right," Tom agreed. "An extinct volcano, luckily for us. And there's the warning device that triggers off the aerial hotfoot."

He pointed to a dish-shaped radar scanner suspended high up near the mouth of the crater.

"What's the other thing?" asked Ed, as he indicated a gleaming conductor which speared up alongside the scanner.

"Probably the antenna that beams out the high-powered electromagnetic radiation," Tom explained. "If we trace the cable connections back through the control board, we'll probably find it's hooked up to the oscillator over there."

Bud scratched his head and turned to his pal with a puzzled frown. "Just one thing I don't savvy, genius boy."

"What's that?"

"An oscillator needs an electrical power input to make it run. But there's nothing like that down here."

Tom grinned. "Now you're asking the pay-off question, chum. See that corona around the pit? That's your answer, I believe."

He opened his jackknife and reached down into the pit. A mere touch of the blade sent up a shower of sparks! Cautiously the young scientist gouged a small particle out of the ground.

"This is something like mica," said Tom. "You know—the flaky substance that's used in making electrical insulation and condensers."

For the first time, his companions realized that the pit was actually a mineral bed of some kind. The soil was streaked and veined with queer materials, some of which Tom had just dug up on the point of his knife blade. He rubbed the stuff between his fingers, and it flaked away at the touch.

"Do you realize what this mineral bed really is?" Tom asked.

"Sure—a mineral bed." Bud grinned.

"That's not all. It's also a huge, natural battery!"

"*What!*"

The others stared at the young inventor in amazement, then Bud pleaded, "Explain it real simple like, so the rest of us can understand."

"Sure, that'll be easy." Tom smiled. "Notice how this bed is made up of thousands of layers of mica with layers of that steellike material between?"

"Yes."

"That steellike material is cerium, another one of the rare earths. Cerium is what they use in photocells. It makes electricity out of the daylight that pours down through the volcano shaft, and stores it up in the form of chemical energy like a giant battery. I imagine that in olden times, when the storm clouds weren't around here all the time, the charge was even stronger."

Tom's companions were awe-struck by the unique phenomenon. Doc pointed to the cables leading from the control board down into the pit. "Then Strang simply tapped this source of power to run his oscillator!"

"Right," Tom agreed. "What's even more amazing is that the ancient people who lived here took advantage of this phenomenon and used it for light. I think they drilled this crevice to bring in the sunlight."

Ed gaped. "You're implying that this civilization achieved a highly advanced level of scientific know-how thousands of years ago!"

"I admit that it's only a theory, Ed, but why else would they build their city underground? There must be some connection between that fact and this natural battery—otherwise it's too big a coincidence to swallow!"

Unable to refute Tom's reasoning, the others looked in awe at the pit. Finally Bud asked:

"How about that electric shock gun, skipper? Do you think Strang used the same stuff in there?"

"I believe not," Tom replied. "But let's find out for sure."

With deft fingers he took the weapon apart, then burst into laughter. "Strang tried to knock me out with one of my own inventions! This shock gun is powered by a Swift solar-charged battery he must have bought!"

"And it boomeranged!" exclaimed Bud as Ed laughed uproariously. Then, as they quieted down, Ed added, "Too bad when a man with ability to do so much good misuses his talents."

Tom nodded. "Well, let's go," he murmured, as he finished reassembling the shock gun. "We still have to find that deposit of rare earths."

Bud pointed to an opening in the wall, which seemed to lead into still another passageway. Let's try in there. That seems to be the only—"

Tom interrupted him excitedly. "There it is!" With a sweep of his hand, he indicated the whole section of wall around the opening.

His companions rushed forward to examine the wall.

"Smokin' rockets!" Bud yelled.

Like the stone used in the houses and temples, the wall was flecked with rainbow hues. The color effect was provided by fibers of the various rare earths—red, blue-green, yellow, and violet in hue. These were embedded in a matrix of soft volcanic rock.

Tom berated himself. "I should have known that the building stones came from a volcanic source."

The opening in the wall had evidently been scooped out with mining tools. It led into the quarry proper from which the building stones had been cut, untold centuries ago.

"Well, I guess that makes the expedition a howling success all around." Ed Longstreet chuckled, clapping his cousin on the back. "We rescued Bud and Hank, and now this rare earths strike should be a sensation on the scientific newsfront!"

In high spirits, the four started back, Tom's brain seething with plans to make the rare earths available to the whole scientific world.

"What I'd like to know," said Ed, "is what happened to the ancient inhabitants. Did they all die out, or just gradually lose their culture, due to some disaster, and degenerate into these present-day savages, like Chief Ahtumik's tribe?"

"Oh, good night!" Tom broke in with a groan. "We forgot the electric shock gun. I left it on the floor of the radar cave. You fellows stay here and I'll run back and get it!"

"*Don't bother!*" ordered a tall, lanky figure that darted from one of the pyramid houses ahead.

"Hedron!" cried Bud.

"Right you are, my friend," the zoologist sneered. "And here's the shock gun. I picked it up while you dopes were snooping into the quarry."

"Don't bother trying to scare us with that," Tom replied coolly. "You should know by now that we have a way to protect ourselves."

Hedron gave an evil chuckle. "Sorry, my dear young genius, but I'm not relying on this shock gun for a moment. Instead, I have something far more effective—namely, this small but powerful grenade bomb!"

Pulling the grenade from his pocket, Hedron suddenly turned and ran toward the mouth of the tunnel. Once there, he hurled the grenade into the cavern, then disappeared through the exit.

A moment later the underground city was rocked by a terrific explosion!

CHAPTER XXV

A DESPERATE CHANCE

KNOCKED off their feet by the force of the blast, Tom and his companions lay stunned for a few moments. Presently the smoke, dust, and rock fragments settled.

"Anybody hurt?" the young inventor asked, as he picked himself up.

Bud, Ed, and Doc Simpson scrambled to their feet and declared themselves unharmed. But their relief was short-lived.

"The tunnel entrance—it's blocked!" Doc cried out.

Rushing forward, they found the situation even worse than they expected. The opening was closed, not merely by rubble, but by thick slabs of rock, apparently shaken loose from the ceiling.

"Good night!" Bud groaned.

Tom forced himself to keep cool. "Only one thing to do," he remarked calmly. "Look for some other way out."

Splitting up into pairs, they began to skirt the

173

walls of the cavern. Tom and Bud started off to the right, working in a counterclockwise direction. Doc and Ed headed the other way. A short time later they joined forces again in the city plaza. No exit had been located.

"I did find some wall inscriptions," Ed remarked. "They may tell the whole story of this underground city."

"You mean you can translate them?" Bud asked.

"I can try! If I follow the same method Ventris used in cracking the Linear B script from Greece and Crete, it should—"

Tom interrupted his cousin. "If we had time to figure out the symbols, they might show us a secret way out. But, in the meantime, we're in a fix. When Hedron reaches the cave entrance, he'll probably take Chow and the others by surprise, knock out the native guards with the shock gun, and turn his friends loose. They'll have the whole valley at their mercy!"

"You're right!" Bud gulped. "But what can we do?"

"Yes," said Doc ruefully. "We've just found out there's no other exit, and that crevice isn't wide enough for us to climb through."

"Let's see if we can't clear a way out with our bare hands," Tom proposed.

They hurried back to the blockade and began pushing and straining against the fallen slabs with all their strength. Their efforts proved hopeless.

"There *must* be some way out of this mess!" Bud groaned.

Tom said slowly, "There might be *one* other way. Suppose we rig up another antenna from the oscillator and aim it at these fallen slabs. Then we aim our resistorizers, so that the two opposing waves intercept right in front of the slabs. I have a hunch we could produce enough heat to melt an opening through the rock."

Tom's companions broke into loud cheers and Doc added, "Guess you've pulled another one out of your hat, inventor boy!"

"Not so fast," Tom cautioned. "Remember that blast of heat when we used our resistorizers against the shock gun?"

"Do I?" Ed grimaced at the memory of the intense heat. "I felt so much like a grilled hamburger, I was going to ask someone to turn me over!"

"That," said Tom, "was nothing compared to the heat we'll get with this setup. That other time we were just dissipating the energy from a small hand weapon. Now we'll be burning up the full output of energy from a large oscillator. It could turn this whole cavern into a blast furnace!"

As Tom's listeners visualized the effect, their faces fell. "You mean it's hopeless?" Doc asked.

"It is, unless we can figure out an answer to that problem, too."

Scowling in concentration, Tom paced back and forth, his hands plunged deep in his pockets. Suddenly he stopped and snapped his fingers.

"Got it! If we build up a barricade around the slabs, it'll enclose and insulate the heat, and make the burning go even faster! We'll use building rock from the quarry. Heaps of it are lying loose back there."

Quickly he organized the operation. Bud, Ed, and Doc were detailed to haul the soft, light-weight lava rock across the cavern and pile it in place around the fallen slabs blocking the tunnel entrance.

Tom himself undertook to rig up the electrical gear. The aerial antenna used for knocking out aircraft was far above his reach. However, he man-aged to haul down almost the whole length of connecting cable which hooked up the antenna to the oscillator.

From the tip of this cable, he stripped off a yard or more of rubber sheathing, thus making a crude substitute for an antenna. Then he dragged the cable across the cavern floor toward the tunnel entrance.

His friends had already built up part of the en-closing shell of rock. Tom inserted the exposed cable through this shell. Then he collected all the available resistorizers and placed them, too, in the rocky barricade with their switches turned on.

At last the setup was ready, and Tom returned to the radar cave to trip the oscillator switch by hand. The other three accompanied him.

"One thing I didn't tell you," he said grimly. "This setup had better work fast, or we're out of luck."

"What do you mean?" Ed asked.

"When the current starts to melt the rock,"

Tom replied, "it'll start using up all the oxygen in the cavern at a dangerous rate."

"How about the crevice in the volcano?" asked Doc. "We can suck in fresh air that way, can't we?"

Tom nodded. "We'll get *some* from there. But don't forget, the melting process will release gases from the rocks that will flood the cavern. At best, the air coming down the volcano shaft will just be able to dilute those gases. The mixture may not be good enough to breathe."

The group exchanged fearful glances. Then Doc shrugged and spoke for the others. "It's our only chance, so let's go!"

Without a word, Tom reached over to the control board and flicked the switch. The dynamo hummed into action.

Tense moments went by. The atmosphere grew thick and murky with the smoke and fumes from the burning rock. Breathing became more difficult.

Holding his handkerchief over his nose and mouth, Tom suddenly plunged toward the blockade. "I want to see how things are coming along," he called back.

Head down, he plowed forward through the billowing fumes. Several times he staggered and almost fell. His head was reeling. Then, suddenly, he felt a rush of fresh air.

"We're through!" he cried hoarsely. "We're through! Cut the power!"

Bud flipped the switch, then he, Ed, and Doc came racing to join Tom. Together, they tore away the barricade of stones. Beyond, a round hole eighteen inches in diameter had been burned through the rocky barrier.

Waiting only long enough for the hot opening to cool a little, Tom and the others squeezed through the narrow passage. As they neared the outer end of the cave, the confused, noisy sounds of a struggle reached their ears.

"Guess we're not too late after all!" Bud exclaimed.

Reaching the entrance, they saw the dazed snipers lying on the ground in crumpled positions.

"Shock gun!" Tom commented tersely.

Just outside the cave, a hand-to-hand fight was in progress. After mowing down the natives, Hedron had managed to free his friends in the ensuing confusion. His cohorts were now engaged in a wild free-for-all with Hank, Slim, and Chow, whom they outnumbered four to three. But the odds were soon tipped the other way as Tom and his companions waded in, swinging haymakers right and left.

"Here goes double for you!" Bud murmured as he rammed an uppercut to Hedron's chin. The fellow crashed face forward, glassy-eyed.

Bud now glanced at Tom, confronting the figure of Brad Wilkins, who had just given both Slim and Chow a terrific battering. With a bull-like roar, the giant bore down on the young inventor. But Tom agilely ducked his hamlike fists and drove a stiff punch to the man's midriff.

With a groan, the balding goliath went down

"Ooof!" the giant grunted, doubling forward in agony.

As his head came down, Tom's right hand came up in a roundhouse blow that jarred him to his heels. With a groan, the balding goliath went down like a collapsing skyscraper.

In a few minutes the fight was over. The four criminals lay propped in a row against the cliff, securely trussed and glaring sullenly at their captors.

"We'll have the Dutch authorities at Hollandia take over," Tom panted.

Later, from the cycloplane, he radioed the *Sky Queen* and asked Arv Hanson to relay the message.

Half an hour later Hanson called back. "The island police say that they can't get through to you. Will you bring the prisoners to town?"

While the cycloplane was on this errand, with Bud acting as pilot, Tom and Ed busied themselves in the ancient city. The young inventor completely dismantled the radar-triggered air weapon.

When Bud returned, he burst out, "Your new invention is terrific, Tom! The *Drumhawk* practically flies itself, even without the cybertron!"

Tom grinned. "Since you like flying it, how about bringing all the gang here? I believe they'd like to see the underground treasure house."

Bud agreed to do this. On his final trip, he surprised his pal by letting off three unexpected passengers.

"Dad! Sandy! Phyl!" Tom cried happily.

"We were so worried about you we couldn't stay away," Phyl said, giving Tom a long look, as greetings were exchanged. "Just as we landed we learned that you were all right."

"What a relief that was!" added Sandy, and her father nodded.

Tom himself led the group through the tunnel and pointed out the wonders of the mysterious city. When they came upon Ed, who had been studying the wall inscriptions, Longstreet cried out excitedly:

"I think I've cracked this problem. If my translation is correct, the people who lived here, about two thousand years ago, reached one of the highest stages of civilization in the ancient world!"

"From which today's people will benefit," said Mr. Swift, gazing proudly at Tom. "I'd suggest, son, that the next thing you do is try to dissipate the storm clouds that hang over this area and give these natives some glowing sunshine."

"I'll do my best, Dad. In the meantime, the mining of the rare earths can begin."

"Sounds to me like too much time underground," Bud spoke up. "I'll venture a guess that Tom will come up with some kind of an invention that'll take the two of us off on another whale of a trip. And boy, I can't wait!"

"I'll try to oblige," Tom replied, his eyes twinkling, not dreaming that within a short time he would be engrossed in *The Undersea Mountain Mystery*.

As the sightseers stepped from the cave, they became aware of the aroma of cooking meat. When they reached the village, the natives were hurrying about, dressed in furred and feathered jungle finery. Some were holding trays of coconut meat, nuts, and roast pig. Several were dancing their tribal steps to music tapped by players on crude drums or whistled through gourds.

Tom's party stopped and were immediately assigned to seats on the ground near a fire over which hung a roasting pig. Chief Ahtumik, almost unrecognizable in his adornment of paint, fur, feathers, and arrows, strode before the group and bowed low. He handed the young scientist one of the rare earth idols.

The chief then nodded toward Ed Longstreet. To everyone else's surprise, Ahtumik said in halting English:

"Give idol for thank you—eat big feast." The drummers began to tap their instruments lightly and the chanters hummed as their chief went on:

"Tom Swift! He great jungle warrior!"

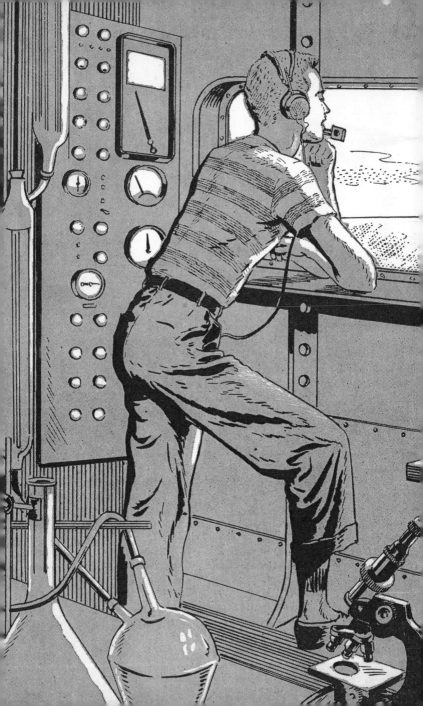